RAVI SUBR

PRESE

A BRUTAL HAND

THERE'S NO ESCAPE

JIGS ASHAR

HarperCollins *Publishers* India

First published in 2020

This edition published in India by HarperCollins *Publishers* in 2023
4th Floor, Tower A, Building No. 10, Phase II, DLF Cyber City,
Gurugram, Haryana – 122002
www.harpercollins.co.in

2 4 6 8 10 9 7 5 3 1

Copyright © Ravi Subramanian 2020, 2023

P-ISBN: 978-93-5629-468-4
E-ISBN: 978-93-5629-469-1

This is a work of fiction and all characters and incidents described in this book are the product of the author's imagination. Any resemblance to actual persons, living or dead, is entirely coincidental.

Ravi Subramanian asserts the moral right
to be identified as the author of this work.

All rights reserved. No part of this publication may be reproduced, stored in a retrieval system, or transmitted, in any form or by any means, electronic, mechanical, photocopying, recording or otherwise, without the prior permission of the publishers.

Typeset by R. Ajith Kumar

Printed and bound at
Replika Press Pvt. Ltd.

MIX
Paper from
responsible sources
FSC® C016779

This book is produced from independently certified FSC® paper to ensure responsible forest management.

A BRUTAL HAND

Celebrating
30 Years of Publishing
in India

Other books in the series

Insomnia
Evoked
Body of Work

NOTE ON RAVI SUBRAMANIAN PRESENTS

For my readers who love pace, I offer *Ravi Subramanian Presents*. I've conceptualised these books as a series of short, plot-oriented, fast paced novellas that are the book equivalent of caffeine for an exhausted mind. These are thrillers on steroids. There isn't a slow moment in these books, not a sentence that does not take the story forward, not a page that doesn't beg to be turned. Airports, railway stations, flights, buses, metros, bedrooms or even behind your laptops—you'd want to read your own copy of these books everywhere. These stories promise to hold you firmly in their grip until you reach the very end.

Ravi Subramanian Presents serves another purpose. I noticed that in our country, mythology and romance are popular genres and draw many capable writers. Crime writing though is often considered too complicated, and has not seen many writers emerge. My co-authors in this series are all brilliant writers, hand-picked by me to fill this gap. Each thriller in this series is written by a talented author with a definite flair for crime writing. It has been a pleasure to work with them and to be able to provide a platform for them.

With short, fast paced, pulse pounding, high impact, no flab stories, *Ravi Subramanian Presents* come with a built in accelerator. So fasten your seatbelts and get ready for the ride!

Ravi Subramanian

ONE

The three men rose from their seats as soon as the end credits started to roll. 'These late-night shows are aptly named,' said one of them as he glanced at his watch. It was 1.30 a.m. when the sparse crowd of around twenty emerged from Carnival Cinemas at Wadala, a central suburb of Mumbai. It was the second, and probably the last, weekend that the thriller, *The Mule* was playing in the city's cinemas. In the era of multiplexes, where movies are released in hundreds of theatres and play on multiple screens at the same time, packed houses are a rarity.

The street outside, illuminated in yellow, was quiet and deserted except for the thin crowd that was now headed towards their cars. The parking lot was behind the theatre complex—a good two-hundred-metre walk through a side lane. Most of the cars were parked outside the theatre to avoid parking fees, and more importantly, the walk to the parking area. Within a few minutes, the silence of the night was broken by the beeps of cars being unlocked, which then sped away along the exit towards the eastern freeway.

The trio, all in their early fifties, stood outside the main exit of the theatre for about twenty minutes, talking animatedly and laughing. Then one of them said, 'Let's call it a night. It's almost two, and I have a long drive home. You guys will be asleep in your beds by the time I reach my car.'

They all laughed and exchanged goodbyes. Two of them walked towards the residential colony to the left of the theatre. The third waved to his friends once more and started walking towards the parking lot. With no streetlamps, the lane was completely dark except for the faint yellow that spilt over from the lights on the main street. He hurried towards the end of the lane and turned right to enter the parking lot. The rectangular parking area could accommodate around thirty cars, fifteen on each side along its length. He spotted his Toyota Camry on the left, nine rows ahead. It was the only car in the lot. *I will park in the front next time,* he said to himself.

A BRUTAL HAND

It was when he unlocked the car with the remote that, in the momentary flickering of light, he thought he saw someone near his car. He waited; but there was no movement, no sound. He relaxed his shoulders and walked briskly towards his car. He opened the door and was about to get in when he heard footsteps behind him. Even as he was turning, an iron rod struck him hard on his head, just above his right ear. Instinctively, he tried to lift his hands towards his bloodied head, but another blow knocked him down. He slumped down against the door and fell to the ground, lifeless, unable to feel the next strike.

TWO

Dr Neel Burman parked his white Audi A3 in the compound of his private clinic in the prime south Mumbai area of Peddar Road. He got out, clutching his Mont Blanc leather briefcase. As was his habit, he checked his Omega; it was a few minutes before 8 a.m.

It was the fifteenth year of his private practice, and he had, without fail, reached his clinic before eight every single day—except on Tuesdays, when he saw patients at the Bombay Government Hospital. He nodded with a slight smile, as if to congratulate himself on his punctuality.

At forty-seven, Neel looked and felt almost ten years younger. He was lean and fit from years of running and tennis, enhancing his conventional good looks—a tall frame, with a chiselled, clean-shaven face.

Neel walked towards the entrance to the building and waved to the familiar security guard. Ignoring the lift, he took the stairs to his clinic on the third floor. He was humming a new Hindi chartbuster as he climbed up, two stairs at a time.

The clinic occupied half the third floor of the seven-storeyed building. *Dr Neel Burman, M.B.B.S., M.D. (Psychiatry)*—announced the nameplate on the main door. Neel opened the door and entered his plush clinic, disabling the security alarm system and switching on the lights and air conditioning, which turned on with a soft buzz.

The clinic opened into a reception area, with a large desk at the centre and a three-seater sofa opposite it. A smaller desk was beside the main one. His secretary, Jaya Shetty, usually arrived by eight-thirty, well before the clinic opened at nine o'clock. Neel preferred coming early to go through his emails and paper mail before the day started.

To the left of the reception was a passage with storage cabinets on both sides. The passage ended with a restroom on one side and a pantry on the other. The pantry had a well-stocked kitchenette, with a mini-refrigerator and a microwave oven. It also had a small dining table with two chairs.

Neel passed through the reception into the waiting area. A soft grey carpet covered the floor; three comfortable brown sofas were placed around a glass centre-table with a few magazines on it. Two bright paintings adorned the opposite walls.

Neel opened the wooden door to his soundproof cabin. His cabin was spacious, with minimalistic furniture—a teakwood desk and a black leather chair on either side. On the desk was a thirty-two-inch monitor, to which he had connected his MacBook. An L-shaped sofa at one end of the room was used for patient consultation. A small table on the other side had a water cooler and a coffee-maker.

He raised the blinds of the French windows, which overlooked a lush green park. Catching sight of his reflection in the glass, he adjusted his neat salt-and-pepper hair. *Not bad*, he thought, admiring himself for a few more seconds. As he turned away, his eyes fell on the distinct inch-long scar on his right temple, and he ran a finger along it.

Neel's thoughts were interrupted by the sound of the clinic's main door opening.

THREE

Inspector Abhay Rastogi was staring at the lifeless body in Carnival Cinema's parking lot. He despised crime, especially murder, and this was the first one in his jurisdiction after a murder-suicide case four months ago. He was in an especially foul mood. He had hoped for a relatively easy day at work after having been on duty for ten days straight. Once again, Rastogi glanced at the smashed, bloodied skull, which made the face almost unrecognisable. He frowned and looked away.

'Did we get the owner's details?' he asked his subordinate, Sub-Inspector Raghav Kadam, pointing to the Toyota's registration plate. They had found no other clue to the victim's identity—no wallet, no car insurance document or any other papers.

'Not yet, should be getting it any minute now,' said Kadam, who had been standing silently behind Rastogi until then. He had worked with Rastogi long enough to know when not to get in his way.

Rastogi shook his head and walked around to the front of the car where two forensic experts were scanning the ground for clues. A police photographer was taking pictures. An iron rod, presumably the murder weapon, had been wrapped in a transparent plastic bag by the forensic team. Rastogi picked the bag up to examine the rod. It was the type commonly used in building construction: around two feet long and an inch in diameter. Its dark grey metal was rusted reddish-brown in a few places, and one end was stained dark brown, where the rod had struck the victim's head.

The police had cordoned off the entire area since the body had been discovered in the early hours of the morning. A resident in a building adjoining the cinema complex had seen the body from his fourth-floor apartment and called the police. By now, most of the nearby buildings had curious onlookers peering through windows and from balconies, some of them pointing their mobile phones at the car, clicking pictures or taking videos. Rastogi looked at them and wondered if any of them would have come forward to help if they had witnessed the killing. Or for that matter, *any* crime. He recalled a recent video posted on YouTube, in which a bystander had *filmed* a woman being raped in broad daylight on a busy street. People were passing by, just watching, not a finger was lifted to help the victim. Rastogi, who had long believed that a police-public partnership could bring crime rates down, was saddened by this state of affairs.

Two media vans had just arrived, and Rastogi could see a television crew setting up their equipment. A few reporters were at the edge of the perimeter set by the police, calling out to Rastogi for a sound byte. He waved to the journalists and had started to walk over to them when he saw Kadam hurrying towards him.

'Just got a call from the road transport team. The car belongs to one Alok Dalal. I have the registered address as well,' Kadam told him.

'Great, let's give the headlines to our friends here,' Rastogi said, pointing to the media, 'and then we need to break the news to the family.'

Rastogi spoke to the reporters for a few minutes and apprised them of the murder, withholding the details about the owner of the car. He did not want to cause any speculation about the victim's identity. Although the car was registered in the name of Alok Dalal, he had to make sure it *was* Alok Dalal who had been murdered before he gave out specifics. He thanked the media and promised to provide them with updates, as and when he had any. Further questions were interrupted by the siren of an ambulance, which was trying to inch its way through the crowd that had gathered at the scene. Rastogi and Kadam moved the barricades to let the ambulance in.

The two police officers and the forensic team watched as two medical professionals stepped down from the ambulance, carrying a stretcher. Used to such sights, they did not bat an eyelid as they went about their business. As they lifted the body and heaved it on to the stretcher, something caught Rastogi's attention.

A post-it note.

Hidden from view so far by the dead man's lifeless hand, the yellow piece of paper was stuck to his shirt sleeve. As the body was lifted, it came off his dangling arm and fell to the ground where the corpse had been lying only moments ago.

Rastogi grimaced, holding his knees as he bent and looked at it. He gestured to Kadam, pinching the air with his index finger and thumb, and then waited with his palm outstretched, much like a surgeon in an operation theatre. Kadam hurried over to the forensic team and returned with a pair of tweezers, which he promptly passed to Rastogi.

The Inspector picked up the yellow note, now smudged brown and red. On it, written in black with a marker pen, was the word 'Sorry'.

FOUR

Jaya Shetty opened the door to the clinic with her set of keys, put her purse on her desk and walked towards Neel's office. She had been the receptionist at Neel's clinic since he began his practice. She was a portly woman of fifty-two, draped in her trademark crisp saree, with her mostly grey hair neatly combed into a bun. Today, as always, not a hair was out of place. Neel often wondered how she managed to appear the way she did, after a gruelling one-hour journey on the local train to work. Jaya lived in Thane, a distant suburb of Mumbai.

She was a single mother who had chosen to walk out of an abusive marriage. Her son was only five at the time. With just basic education, she had been struggling to make ends meet when she applied for the post of receptionist at Neel's clinic. That was a decade and a half ago. Although there were more qualified applicants, Neel was particularly impressed with her bold, decisive personality, and decided to give her the job. He also supported the education of her only son, Gaurav, who was now twenty and in his final year of graduation. Gaurav often dropped in to meet Neel for advice on his studies and career. Neel was quite fond of him and treated him like family.

Neel had started his practice in a rented flat in an old building in Girgaum, around two kilometres from his new clinic. It was a time when psychiatrists were not in high demand, as they are today. However, while the number of patients opting for psychiatric help had increased over the years, one thing did not change—the patients' need for anonymity. Hardly anyone spoke about the professional treatment they were undergoing for their mental health. Neel found that very strange. For him, going to a psychiatrist was like going to any other doctor, such as a dentist. If you have a problem, solve it, he believed.

In any case, Neel was not complaining. His practice was thriving, although he did feel a bit guilty at times about the fact that his success was dependent on others' problems. But that is true for most professions, he would reason with himself.

'Good morning, Doctor.' Jaya greeted him with a warm smile.

'Morning, Jaya.'

'Shall we go through the letters?'

'Sure, let's get started.' Neel smiled as he sat down with the newspaper and a cup of coffee. Jaya took the stack of envelopes and sat down opposite Neel. On most occasions, Neel handled his mail himself; but if Jaya came in before he started with it, he preferred to sit back and enjoy his coffee. Jaya put on her reading glasses and went through the mail quickly, glancing at each envelope just for a few seconds, not even opening most of them. She put aside the electricity bill, gave the bank statements to Neel and consigned the rest of the papers to the shredder.

'Nothing?' asked Neel, raising his eyebrows.

'No, just the usual,' she replied.

'Great, how is the day scheduled?'

'Two patients. Mrs Khanna has her monthly appointment at ten, and then a first visit by Tarun Malhotra, the actor.'

'Tarun Malhotra?' asked Neel, surprised.

'Yes, just five years in Bollywood, and he needs help.'

'Must be his string of flops,' laughed Neel. 'By the

way, where is Manohar these days? I haven't seen him the whole of last week.'

'I have no idea where he is. Must be up to one of his useless get-rich-quick schemes,' Jaya said. 'You should not have hired him, in my opinion. We are not sure if he—'

'Come on, Jaya. He has paid his price; three years in prison is a long time,' Neel said.

'But ... I just don't trust him. There is something about him that makes me very nervous.'

'Everyone deserves a second chance, Jaya.'

FIVE

Rastogi and Kadam reached the address to which the Toyota was registered. They got out of the police car and looked up at the high-rise, Hill Crest. The twenty-storeyed building was on a gentle slope at Walkeshwar, a sea-facing area in South Mumbai. Seeing the two men in uniform approaching the gate, the security guard jumped to his feet and opened it, giving them a clumsy salute. He stared nervously at the tall, scrawny Kadam, and then at stout and balding Rastogi.

Twirling his thick moustache, Rastogi asked the security guard in a stern voice, 'Which floor does Alok Dalal stay on?'

'Top floor,' stuttered the guard.

'Does he own a Toyota Camry?' continued Rastogi.

'Yes, sir.'

'Is it parked somewhere here? Can you show it to me?'

'No, sir. Alok Sir took the car last night but has not returned yet.'

Rastogi nodded and without another word, started for the elevator. Once they were inside, Kadam pressed 20 on the panel and the elevator whirred into action, stopping directly at the twentieth floor. The doors opened to the foyer, which was like a five-star hotel lobby—well-lit, with Italian marble flooring. To the right were two armchairs and a chaise lounge.

'The foyer is bigger than my entire house,' Kadam chuckled, looking around.

Rastogi ignored the comment, looked up at the CCTV camera and rang the doorbell.

SIX

An attractive lady in her late forties, dressed in an elegant blue salwar-kameez, opened the door. She showed signs of curiosity but no surprise on seeing the cops at her doorstep. *The security guard must have announced our arrival,* thought Rastogi.

'Hello, I am Inspector Abhay Rastogi, and this is my colleague, Raghav Kadam,' Rastogi said.

'I am Madhoo Dalal. How can I help you? Is something wrong?' she asked.

'May we come in, please?' Rastogi said and entered the lavish apartment.

Rastogi and Kadam sat next to each other on the comfortable sofa in the living area; Madhoo on a leather chair opposite them, looking at them expectantly.

Rastogi started, 'Alok Dalal ...'

'Is my husband ... what's the matter?' Madhoo asked.

'Where is Mr Dalal at the moment?'

'He ... must be at his office, I think.'

'And when did you see him last?'

'Last evening. He came home from work and told me he was going to watch a movie with his friends. I left immediately after to visit my parents.'

'And did he return home last night?' Rastogi pursued.

'I presume so ... I stayed over at my parents', and I just got back home. I thought he had left for office. Is anything wrong, Inspector?'

Rastogi looked at Kadam, sighed and continued, 'I hope it's all a mistake ... but—'

'But what?'

Just as Rastogi was about to say something, a young girl who bore a striking resemblance to Madhoo Dalal entered the living room. She stood behind Madhoo's chair, looking at them nervously.

'This is my daughter, Nitya,' Madhoo said.

'Mom, why are they here?' Nitya asked, without greeting them.

Rastogi looked at Madhoo, unsure whether to speak in front of Nitya, who he guessed was in her late teens. Madhoo nodded at him to continue.

'We have found a body, lying next to your husband's car,' Rastogi said as gently as he could. He saw Nitya grip her mother's shoulders, looking terrified. Madhoo placed her right hand on Nitya's, her gaze fixed on Rastogi.

'Is it—?' Madhoo asked.

'We are not sure, Mrs Dalal. We would like you to come with us and identify the body.'

Tears welled up in Madhoo's eyes as she looked up at Nitya, who was staring blankly at the wall behind Rastogi.

SEVEN

It *was* Alok Dalal who had been brutally murdered; his identity was confirmed by Madhoo. A few friends of the Dalals had reached the morgue to be with the family. Rastogi had questions but reserved them for a later time. He expressed his condolences to Madhoo and Nitya and left for Wadala police station, where he had been the station-in-charge for the past four years. With Kadam at the wheel, Rastogi made a few calls—a couple of them to his key contacts in the media to confirm the name of the victim, and one to the zonal-in-charge, his boss, to keep him updated.

It was almost lunchtime when they reached the police station. Rastogi entered his office, walking at a surprisingly brisk pace for his bulk, and sat down at his desk. Kadam followed him inside and stood beside his desk, waiting for instructions.

'I want to know everything about Alok Dalal. Ten minutes,' he said to Kadam.

'Yes, sir,' said Kadam as he rushed out.

Rastogi closed his eyes to process all the information he had on the case.

Was Alok Dalal killed for his wallet? It was missing. But so were the car's documents. So, was it for the money, or to hide the victim's identity? But the car registration plate would have given it away anyway.

And the 'Sorry' card? Was it already lying there when Dalal was attacked? Or was it placed there by the killer? Was the killer trying to convey that he, or she, was sorry for committing the murder? It was unlikely that the killer was a she; the blows to the head were too forceful, too brutal. But he had been surprised before in this regard.

Rastogi shook his head and opened his eyes. Realising he had not eaten anything since the morning, he stepped out of the police station and went across the road to Poornima Lunch Home, a small joint which served South Indian food. As he sat at his regular table, the waiter, without waiting for his order, put a plate of idli-sambhar and a filter coffee in front of him. This was Rastogi's lunch on most days, and also his dinner for a few days in a week. At fifty-three, Rastogi was a bachelor who lived alone, and he could not remember the last time he had used a cooking stove. Having finished his meal, he was about to get up when Kadam walked in.

'Yes, Kadam?' Rastogi said, gesturing to the waiter to get the same order for his colleague.

'Sir, Alok Dalal is ... was ... one of the leading diamond merchants in Mumbai. A third-generation jeweller, he is largely responsible for expanding his family's business globally, setting up offices in London and Amsterdam. He has one sibling—an elder sister who married an NRI and lives in Singapore.'

Rastogi was listening intently, eyes closed and hands folded below his chin.

'Recently, he opened retail showrooms in India and London. Apparently, that venture did not take off, and he incurred huge losses. The word on the street is that he defaulted on his payments to lenders within the trade.'

'And that is not forgiven in this business,' said Rastogi, opening his eyes.

EIGHT

'*Where are you hiding, little one? Come to me.*'
The soft, sing-song voice echoed in the darkness. Young eyes stared from below the bed, wide awake and terrified. What if heartbeats were loud enough to give away the hiding place? The footsteps seemed to fade away, but only for a moment. And then, the familiar creak of the door opening. Black leather shoes, shining and spotless, entered the room, moving around, searching.

'*Come out ... wherever you are. I will count to three. One ...*'

The feet were angry now, moving faster. They stopped in front of the wardrobe, which was pulled open with a loud noise.

'*Two ... are you in the garden, little one?*'

A BRUTAL HAND

The unblinking little eyes saw the shoes turn suddenly and move towards the door, closing in relief as the door opened again, already relaxing into sleep in the cold safety of the hiding place.

'Three!' came the scream as a strong hand grabbed the tiny legs.

The dreamer woke up in a cold sweat. That familiar nightmare, refusing to let go, night after night.

When will you leave me alone?

The killer took a sip of cold water from a glass by the bedside.

NINE

'You are doing great, Mr Karnik. I don't think you need to take the medicines anymore,' said Neel, smiling, as he walked his patient, Nitin Karnik, to the door. Karnik, a renowned hotelier in his mid-seventies, had been consulting Neel for the last three years. He had been overcome by a paranoid fear that his family was trying to poison him. Neel, who knew the family well, had worked hard, using a combination of psychotherapy and medication to cure the septuagenarian of his suspicion.

'But I can still come and talk to you, right?' The old man was almost pleading.

'Of course you can, but not as a patient,' laughed Neel.

'Thank you, doctor,' Nitin said, taking Neel's hands in his.

'Goodbye, and take care,' said Neel.

Jaya smiled at him as he turned back from the door and said, 'You should get going now.'

Neel looked at his watch. 'This early? It's just about five.'

'You have a dinner date, remember?'

'Oh, yes! Thanks for reminding me. What would I do without you, Jaya?'

Just then, the door opened, and a greasy-haired young man of average height walked into the clinic. He was sporting a stubble, and the narrow eyes under his thick eyebrows were red, as if he had not slept for days. He looked at Neel and grunted, ignoring Jaya.

'Where have you been, Manohar?' Jaya asked.

Manohar Rao worked at Neel's clinic as an assistant, filing documents, taking care of the pantry and running errands. He was also tasked with opening the clinic with his set of keys and cleaning it before Neel arrived. However, on most days if not all, he came into work long after both Neel and Jaya.

'Are you alright, Manohar?' Neel asked.

'I am fine, doctor.'

Neel looked him in the eye. 'Are you sure you're not in any trouble?'

'Yes, doctor. No trouble at all. Why do you ask?' Manohar smiled.

TEN

Neel reached his apartment complex in Worli and parked his car in its slot in the basement of the newly constructed building. The four-kilometre drive from his clinic had taken less than fifteen minutes as he had managed to beat the peak-hour traffic that evening. He rang the doorbell of his apartment, which occupied the entire seventh floor, and adjusted the alignment of a painting on the wall of the foyer as he waited.

'Hello, beautiful,' he said cheerfully as Charu, his wife, opened the door with a look of amazement on her face.

'You actually came early!' she said, giving Neel a warm hug.

'Of course, how could I forget our dinner date?'

Charu looked askance at Neel and laughed. 'Jaya reminded you, didn't she?'

'Umm ... no ... I remembered,' said Neel, and grinned. 'Yeah, actually she did.'

'Let me get you a coffee,' Charu said and went to the kitchen.

Rolling up his sleeves, Neel walked slowly through the tastefully decorated living area and stepped on to the wide balcony. He could see a half-full cup of coffee, still steaming, on a wrought iron table in the balcony. A book on gardening lay open next to it. He saw Charu coming his way and smiled. She still looked the same as she did when they had gotten married, twenty years ago—tall, slim and extremely pretty. She blushed, her brown eyes twinkling as she caught him looking at her and gave him a dazzling smile. Most people had trouble believing that she was the mother of a sixteen-year-old, their daughter Inaaya.

'Here you are.' Charu handed Neel a hot cup of black coffee, just the way he liked it.

'Thanks. How was your day?' Neel asked.

'Great. I am ready with the first draft; did the edits today,' Charu replied.

'So, when do I get to read your next bestseller?'

'I have already made a printout for you. Give me your comments so I can make the changes.'

'Sure, I will.' Neel smiled.

After finishing her MBA, Charu had worked with a leading multinational bank as an investment banker. She and Neel had met at a friend's party. They hit it off right away, and after a month of dating, Neel had proposed. And within a minute Charu had said yes. She had taken to writing five years back as a hobby, but it soon consumed her. After her first book became a national bestseller, she gave up her job and began to write full-time. Her second and third books were bestsellers too, firmly establishing her as one of the leading crime writers in the country. Neel often wondered how such a gentle, loving person could produce the violent thrillers she wrote.

'So, where are you taking me, Mr Burman?' Charu asked, snuggling up to Neel.

'It's a surprise.' He smiled and kissed her.

ELEVEN

As Neel and Charu opened the door of their apartment to leave, Inaaya stepped out of the elevator. A petite, bespectacled version of Charu, she was dressed casually in denims and a loose t-shirt. Having just appeared for her tenth standard exams, Inaaya was doing a part-time internship with Mercedes Benz in the mornings and learning Mandarin at the Chinese Language Institute in the evenings. She was chatting on the phone now and did not notice her parents until they were right in front of her.

'Oh, hi,' she said, removing her earphones.

'Hi, sweetheart,' Neel said, giving her a hug. 'We are going out for dinner. You want to join us?'

'No, too boring. I'll order in,' Inaaya said as she went inside the apartment, resuming her chat.

Neel looked at Charu, rolled his eyes and shrugged. She smiled.

'Has she spoken to you about what she wants to do next?' Neel asked Charu as he eased his car out on to the driveway.

'Still uncertain. But she wants to pursue her graduation abroad, not in India.' Charu said.

'Only two years before she flies out of the nest then.'

'She will be fine. Don't worry.' Charu put her hand over Neel's.

They drove in silence for the next twenty minutes, listening to old Hindi songs that they both loved.

'At least now you can tell me where we're going?'

'That will kill the surprise.'

After a few minutes, as Neel turned right at the High Court junction, Charu smiled. 'Wasabi, my favourite!'

Neel grinned.

TWELVE

The murder of Alok Dalal was the main story headlining all television news channels and newspapers. Rastogi had activated his network of informants throughout the city and was hoping for a lead. It had been more than forty-eight hours since the killing, but he had not made any headway in the case. *Have to crack this case in the next couple of days*, Rastogi told himself, knowing full well that the colder a case gets, the more difficult it is to solve.

It was time to have a conversation with Madhoo Dalal. The prayer meeting for Alok Dalal had been held that evening, and Rastogi knew the family would be home afterwards. It was past 8 p.m. when he reached the Dalal residence. An unknown man—a relative,

Rastogi presumed—opened the door and led him inside. There were six people in the living area, in addition to Madhoo Dalal. *Close family and friends,* thought Rastogi. There was silence when they recognised the Inspector, who greeted them with folded hands, expressing his condolences. Some of them started to get up, but Madhoo gestured to them to remain seated.

'Shall we sit in the other room?' Madhoo led Rastogi through a wide corridor. He followed her, admiring the artefacts and paintings along the way. Ahead of him, he saw a door left slightly ajar. Madhoo looked inside with a stern expression before pulling the door shut. As Rastogi passed the closing door, he caught a glimpse of Nitya lounging on a beanbag, earphones in, laughing and chatting on her phone.

Madhoo entered a room at the end of the passage and switched on the lights. It was a well-appointed study, containing a desk with a laptop and a large monitor, a leather chair and a reclining sofa. A bookshelf occupied an entire wall, and french windows overlooked the Arabian Sea on the opposite side. Rastogi sat down next to Madhoo on the sofa.

'I know it is a difficult time, but I wanted to ask a few questions, if that's fine with you?'

'I understand, Inspector. You have to do your job, and I would like you to catch whoever—' Madhoo said, her voice choking.

Rastogi gave her a minute to compose herself before he asked, 'Did your husband have any enemies? You know, bitter rivalry in business, or some such thing?'

'None that I know of.'

'Can you think of any motive that anyone could have to ... to take such drastic action?'

Madhoo shook her head.

'Is it true that Mr Dalal had incurred losses in his new business venture? And that he was burdened with a huge debt?'

'Yes, that's true. But then, these things happen in business. And he did not seem stressed about it. Also, he had borrowed money from close friends and business associates, people we have known for years. I don't think any of them—' Madhoo trailed off.

Rastogi nodded. 'We would like to look at Mr Dalal's emails and phone records. All his postal correspondence as well. We will also be asking a few questions at his office. I trust that is fine?'

'Sure, Inspector. Whatever help you need.'

'Thank you, Mrs Dalal. I would like to take the

phones, laptop and other mail with me right now, if you don't mind.'

'Give me a few minutes,' Madhoo went out of the room and soon returned, carrying two mobile phones and a stack of envelopes, which she placed on the desk. She then took a brown leather briefcase out of a drawer and put the laptop, phones and documents in it. 'And these are the passwords,' she said, sticking a post-it note on the laptop.

'Thank you, Mrs Dalal.' Rastogi's eyes were riveted on the post-it note as he zipped the briefcase and rose to leave.

Madhoo followed him out of the study. As Rastogi passed Nitya's room, he turned and asked, 'How has she taken it? Her father's death?'

'She is very upset. She was very close to him.'

Rastogi looked at Madhoo for a few moments and glanced at Nitya's closed door. 'Can I speak to your daughter?'

THIRTEEN

Nitya turned to face the door when she heard it open. She was still sprawled on her beanbag. 'Talk later,' she said on the phone and hung up, as Rastogi and Madhoo stepped into the room. She sat up and looked at her mother questioningly.

'Hello, Nitya. I am Inspector Abhay Rastogi. I know it's a difficult time, but I would like to speak with you regarding—'

'I understand, Inspector,' Nitya cut him short, and looked up at him. *Go on, she seemed to suggest.*

Rastogi sat down on a black study chair. To his disappointment, Madhoo sat down on the bed next to Nitya's beanbag. He had wanted to speak to Nitya alone but decided against asking her mother to leave the room, considering the delicate situation.

'Okay, coming straight to the point, is there anyone you can think of who could have murdered your father?'

'He was ...' she started but stopped abruptly and looked fixedly at the phone lying next to her. Rastogi looked at her expectantly and then at Madhoo, who put her hand gently on Nitya's. The soft touch was in complete contrast to the stern, almost angry expression that flickered on her face as she looked at her daughter. Although it was only for a fleeting moment, Rastogi did not miss it.

Nitya teared up, sniffed and looked at the Inspector.

'No, I cannot think of anyone,' she said.

FOURTEEN

At 6:30 p.m., right on schedule, lights were switched off in the Byculla Women's Prison at Nagpada in central Mumbai. Jail Superintendent Ramakant Deshmukh changed out of his uniform, pocketed his mobile phone and some cash, and called it a day. At six-foot-one, he had to stoop as he moved his burly frame out of his office door. His bulging eyes, under bushy eyebrows, were bloodshot; Deshmukh had not slept for the last three nights.

As he walked towards the exit, Deshmukh gestured to Arun Bapat, his second-in-command.

'Yes, sir,' said Bapat, rushing towards Deshmukh.

'All set for tomorrow?'

'Yes, sir.'

'I do not want any problems to arise. Have you taken

care of 106?' Deshmukh asked, referring to an inmate by her designated prison number.

'Yes, I have spoken to her. If she does not behave, she knows what will happen,' Bapat said.

Deshmukh nodded, continuing, 'And I want one more round of cleaning to happen tonight. This place has to look like a hotel.'

'We are on it, sir.'

'Good,' said Deshmukh as he stepped out of the main gate. Before Bapat could close the gate, Deshmukh turned around. 'And the catering?'

'Arranged, sir.'

Deshmukh waved to Bapat, who nodded and closed the gate. The Jail Superintendent stood outside the closed gate, going through his mental checklist for the next day's visit. Next month, he would be completing his eleventh year as head of the Byculla Women's Prison. *I hope I live to see the day,* thought Deshmukh.

FIFTEEN

For eleven years, Deshmukh had ruled over Byculla Women's Prison as if it were his fiefdom and treated the three hundred inmates as his slaves. He had created a coterie of like-minded jail staff, all of whom agreed to his way of running the prison. At the slightest hint of a complaint—be it about food, space or hygiene—the jail officials would beat up the inmates, under Deshmukh's supervision. The younger and prettier inmates were taken care of personally by Deshmukh. And he was very vocal about the consequences of any resistance on the part of the inmates to his methods: *If you want to survive, don't utter a word.*

The trouble in Deshmukh's paradise had started about a year earlier, when a high-profile socialite was transferred there. A month after she was jailed, she moved court, alleging that she had been beaten up by the jail authorities and also been subjected to sexual assault. Her lawyer used the media well and garnered the support of a few NGOs. Soon, Byculla Women's Prison made national headlines.

Unfortunately for Deshmukh, the bigger problem was that the incident had sparked off a rebellion within the prison. On one such occasion, ten months ago, during lunch hour, three inmates complained to the jail staff about the worms they had found in the food. The jail officials responded in the only manner they knew, by thrashing the three women. United by their newfound aggression, more than thirty women prisoners had retaliated, beating up the jail staff. Outnumbered by the rampaging women, Deshmukh and his men had to call in the Riot Control Police.

The prison riot got the attention of the State Human Rights Commission, which ordered an inquiry into the incident. Deshmukh used his connections to stall the progress of the inquiry. Within six months, he also got the socialite transferred to another prison, citing threats to her life from other inmates. Since then, he had been trying to re-establish his former control over the inmates, and while he was largely successful, a few sporadic incidents had kept him on his toes.

Deshmukh was just beginning to settle back into his old routine when he received a letter from the Inspector General of Prisons. The letter announced that the rioting incident was brought up in Parliament by a woman MP, who also demanded a complete revamp of prisons for women in the country. Among other proposals, the main demand was for all-women staff, including the superintendent, in women's prisons.

To assess the conditions first-hand, ten women parliamentarians were scheduled to visit the Byculla Women's Prison. This visit would take place on the following day, and for the first time in his thirty-year career, Deshmukh was worried. While a transfer was a distinct possibility, and one that he was prepared for, he feared that things would get much worse if one of the inmates opened her mouth in front of the delegation.

That would be curtains for him.

SIXTEEN

Deshmukh reached his quarters, which were only a short walk from the prison, and entered his two-room flat. Since his divorce a few years back, he had been living alone. He desperately needed a drink, but he also wanted to appear at his best for the delegation the next morning. After a brief inner debate, he made up his mind. *Only one drink,* he promised himself.

He walked slowly to the Byculla railway station and boarded a northbound local train on the Central main line. The second main line of the Mumbai suburban railways is the Western line, and the third is the Harbour line. Together, these three lines form the local railway network of Mumbai and are often referred to as the 'lifeline' of the city, virtually bringing the metropolis to a halt when they malfunction on a few occasions every year. He got down at Matunga in central Mumbai, five stations from Byculla. It had recently entered the record books as the first suburban railway station in India to be completely staffed by women.

It was 9 p.m. on a Sunday and the trains were almost empty. As Matunga was not a connecting junction, there were very few people across the station's four platforms at this time. Deshmukh climbed the stairs to the foot overbridge and turned left to commence a five-hundred-metre walk along the infamous Z-bridge that connected Matunga station on the Central line to Matunga Road station on the Western line. The bridge was walled on both sides by seven-foot-high asbestos sheets, with the open skies for a ceiling. Steel railings ran across its length on both sides, at a height of around four feet.

The Z-bridge had been rated the most unsafe pedestrian bridge in Mumbai, in a recent study conducted by an NGO. However, in spite of its desolate air and unsavoury reputation, the bridge was often used by commuters as it shortened the distance between the two suburbs considerably, not to mention the fact that the stations it connected provided access to popular areas on both its sides. Some months earlier, students from a few Mumbai colleges had undertaken 'safety walks' during the nights to make the commuters, especially women, feel safer. However, this was a short-lived measure and did nothing to increase commuter confidence.

That night, the only people on the Z-bridge other than Deshmukh were a couple walking in the opposite direction. They hastened their pace as they approached Deshmukh and hurried away. Deshmukh looked across the bridge at the railway carriage workshop, and then at his watch. He was eager to meet his friends at their usual drinking hole, a local bar called Prithvi, a short distance from Matunga Road station.

Deshmukh entered the bar, waved to the cashier and looked around. The place was drab and seedy, a row of tables lining its length on either side. The darkness inside was worsened by the cigarette smoke, and stank of cheap alcohol. Two waiters paced up and down the narrow aisle. One of them saw Deshmukh and gestured to a table further down, where his group of drinking mates were sitting. The trio cheered loudly as Deshmukh approached. He took a swig of whiskey from a bottle on the table as he sat down. Deshmukh could barely hear what his friends were saying to him, but that did not matter. He was glad to get his mind off the next day's inspection.

Deshmukh was five drinks down when he looked at his watch again. Eleven-thirty. He decided it was time to leave. He gulped down a final drink, staggered up, and with a quick goodbye, left. He did not bother to pay his share.

He walked slowly, swaying slightly as he started to cross the Z-bridge. There was not a soul in sight. He had just taken the first turn on the bridge, which was shaped like the alphabet it was named after, when he heard a clink behind him: the sound of a hard object hitting the metal railing.

Deshmukh looked over his shoulder without slowing his pace and saw a person bending down, apparently to tie their shoelaces. There was no one else in sight. He shrugged, assuming that the sound had come from the carriage workshop, and continued his walk. In another three minutes, he took the next turn. When he heard the sound again, this time louder. He stopped at the corner after making the turn, leaning on the asbestos sheet. He was waiting for the person behind him to pass by. Silence. He realised he was sweating, although there was a nip in the air.

He waited for a minute, though it seemed much longer. Then, slowly, he retraced his steps around the corner he had just taken. As soon as he made the turn, he saw a hooded figure in black, right in front of him. Before Deshmukh could say or do anything, the figure lifted a rod, and in a flash, it came crashing down on his head. Deshmukh fell to his knees, his head now at the waist of the assailant. He tried to open his eyes but his vision was blurry, partly because of the blood streaming down his face, and partly due to the pain. But he heard the swish of the rod as it cut sharply through the air before it hit him again, smashing the back of his skull.

Deshmukh stayed on his knees—already dead—for a few seconds, before falling on his face.

SEVENTEEN

So this is how you feel just before you die, thought the ten-year-old, all the while trying frantically to escape drowning. The small, feeble hands were tired of fighting the iron grip that was pushing the child's head below the icy water. The four-foot drum seemed mightier than the ocean, and the young, naked body could feel the water closing in from all sides inside it. The head filled with a silent scream as the last gasp drew in water, and the tiny hands stopped splashing.

The slight body was pulled out of the water with a sudden jerk by the now-familiar rough hand, the metal bracelet around the thick, hairy wrist, clattering against the inside of the drum. And then the laughter.

Surprisingly, for all the fear of drowning in the drum,

the first thought in the young mind was, 'Why did he pull me up?'

'Let me go!' the killer screamed, and then realised it was the old haunting nightmare.

Have I not killed you yet?

EIGHTEEN

Rastogi stepped out of the elevator of the Panchratna building near Charni Road and walked to the waiting police car. He had just finished the last of his meetings with Alok Dalal's business associates. The Panchratna building is a Mumbai landmark, having housed the city's diamond bourse for decades before the market shifted to the central business district of Bandra-Kurla Complex. A handful of diamond merchants, mostly old-timers, still operated from a few offices in the building. The rest of the space was now occupied by various other businesses.

Rastogi sat down in the passenger seat of the car and opened his black diary. He scrolled down a list of names to the eleventh number and struck it off. This was the final interview from the list he had prepared, after having gone through Alok Dalal's mobile records, emails and letters. He looked up at Kadam and shook his head. *Three months and nothing to show.*

Rastogi had taken the help of a colleague and friend in the Cyber Crime Investigation Cell to search Dalal's email and phone data. Although he had the passwords and could access the dead man's devices, he wanted to check the records for the previous six months, and wished to have technical expertise at hand, in case he needed it.

He had been optimistic that he could crack the case by following up on the debt angle, but that turned out to be a non-starter. The loans were secured by Alok Dalal's property and other assets. It did not look like Dalal was a man who had made any enemies, unless he had been hiding something. *Was it a random killing, and Alok Dalal merely an unfortunate victim? Or was he missing something?*

'Let's go,' he told Kadam.

They were about to reach the police station when Rastogi's phone buzzed. It was the commissioner's office.

'Yes, sir,' Rastogi answered, wondering what excuse he could possibly give the Commissioner for not having made any headway in the case.

'Rastogi, Commissioner Bedi here.'

'Good morning, sir.'

'Have you heard about the murder?'

'Where? When, sir?'

'Today. Z-Bridge.'

'No, sir, I didn't hear anything about it.'

'I want you to handle the case,' the Commissioner said.

'But, sir …'

'I know it is not in your jurisdiction. But it is *your* case.'

'I am sorry, sir. I don't understand …'

'We found a post-it near the dead body, with "*Sorry*" written on it.'

NINETEEN

Rastogi reached the Matunga police station and headed straight for the station-in-charge's office. Vilas Pendse was an old-timer; he and Rastogi went back a long way. Pendse shook Rastogi's hand, a wry smile on his face. A serial killer is every cop's worst nightmare.

'I know why you are here … got a call from the commissioner's office,' Pendse said as they both sat down.

'Who is the victim?' Rastogi asked.

'Well, it's someone we both knew. Ramakant Deshmukh.'

'Deshmukh? Byculla Women's Prison?'

Pendse nodded. Rastogi let out a long whistle. They both sat in silence for a few minutes, each one aware of what the other was thinking. There was a knock at the door that jolted both of them out of the silence. Pendse looked up and waved in the pantry boy, who laid two cups of tea and a plate of biscuits on the desk. Rastogi helped himself to one.

As he sipped the tea, Rastogi said, 'I would like to see the evidence.'

'Of course, you can take it. It's *your* case now,' Pendse said, grinning.

'Bastard,' Rastogi said, and they both laughed.

TWENTY

It was 11 p.m., but Rastogi was still in his office. He sat at his desk, eyes closed, nodding or shaking his head from time to time. Someone who did not know Rastogi would wonder at his behaviour, but his staff had worked with him long enough to know he was busy thinking. Analysing. Trying to connect the dots, and today it was the two cases. His black diary lay open before him, with its neatly hand-written notes. The modus operandi and the post-it notes suggested it was the same killer. But he could not figure out any connection between the two victims.

Alok Dalal. Diamond merchant. Family man. Clean image.

Ramakant Deshmukh. Jail superintendent. Loner. Tyrant.

Rastogi sighed. He knew about Deshmukh. Everyone in the police force did. His atrocities were no secret, and Rastogi found it appalling that no action had been taken to bring him to book. Despite the inquiry, the court case and the human rights activism, Deshmukh's evil had continued unabated. At one level, Rastogi was glad Deshmukh had met the fate he had. But he quickly dismissed those thoughts. *Get on with your duty,* he told himself.

And then something struck him. There seemed to be no identifiable motive, so far, for Dalal's killing. But Deshmukh was a different story. The motives were all there—too many of them, in fact. Many people would have wanted Deshmukh dead. He just had to find out who was desperate enough to do it.

TWENTY-ONE

'Thank you for the information. It was very useful,' Rastogi told Bapat, Deshmukh's trusted officer, now the interim in-charge at the prison. They were seated in the Jail Superintendent's office, where a garlanded photograph of Deshmukh had been hung on the wall behind his desk. Rastogi finished his tea and stood up, with some difficulty, to leave. Kadam followed suit.

'So, to summarize our discussion,' Rastogi said, looking at Bapat, 'there is nobody who may have had a motive to kill Deshmukh. He was a do-gooder, unable to hurt a fly.'

'Yes, sir,' Bapat said, with a straight face. Either Rastogi's sarcasm was lost on him, or he was an excellent actor. 'Actually,' Rastogi said, as he sat down again, 'I would also like to speak to a few inmates.'

Bapat's face changed colour, turning pale in record time.

TWENTY-TWO

'I will take it from here,' Rastogi told Bapat as a middle-aged woman clad in a white saree with a blue border walked into Deshmukh's office. She made no eye contact with Bapat as she passed him, but Rastogi could sense the palpable tension in her body language, which he attributed to fear. Bapat did not move, stubbornly rooted to his seat. Kadam moved forward and gently, but firmly, led Bapat away, despite his meek protests.

'Have a seat, please,' Rastogi said, pointing to a chair opposite his. Rastogi had selected three inmates, going through the prison register he had taken from Bapat. Given Bapat's lies about Deshmukh's conduct, he wanted to ensure an independent selection of his interviewees.

The woman sat down, hands clasped, looking at the floor. Rastogi had read her file before calling her in. *Sarita Borkar. Age: 33 years. Serving her seventh year, sentenced to ten. Convicted for drug dealing. She had refuted all charges.*

'So, Ms Borkar ... may I call you Sarita?' Rastogi asked gently.

The woman nodded.

'Thank you. My name is Abhay Rastogi, and I am investigating the murder of Ramakant Deshmukh,' Rastogi paused, waiting for a reaction. There was none. He went on. 'Can you tell me about him? I mean, how did he treat you, the inmates here? Anything about his officers? Something that can help us get a lead on the person who murdered him ...'

Sarita did not say anything but looked up at Rastogi hesitantly.

'Go on, Sarita. Do not be afraid. I am on your side. Nobody will know what you tell me,' Rastogi said, leaning slightly forward.

'But ...' Sarita started, and then looked over her shoulder at the door.

Rastogi understood why she was frightened. 'Don't worry about Bapat. I will handle him,' he said in a reassuring tone. Sarita stared at him for a few seconds, unable to make up her mind. Finally, she sighed and said, 'I am glad he is dead.'

TWENTY-THREE

For the next hour, Rastogi listened intently as Sarita narrated the horrors of life at Byculla Women's Prison. Her eyes often welled with tears, and her voice was sad and angry at the same time. Assaults by the jail officers, both physical and sexual, were a daily routine at the prison. The inmates saw a ray of hope when the State Human Rights Commission had gotten involved a year back, but after no action was taken for months, Deshmukh resumed his atrocities—this time, wreaking havoc with a vengeance.

Sarita was trembling when she finished her story. Rastogi, eyes closed, was shaking his head slowly, dismayed at what one of his own had been doing. He offered a glass of water to Sarita, who took it with shaking hands and had a sip.

'I am sorry for what all of you have suffered here. But I have to do my job. I hope you understand that?' Rastogi said.

Sarita nodded and looked up. 'Is there anything else, Inspector?'

'While I do not approve of anyone taking the law into his or her hands, least of all by killing someone, I understand there may be a lot of people who wanted to kill Deshmukh. And given what he has done here, maybe it is someone related to an inmate? Or someone who got released from here? Is that possible?'

'Entirely possible,' said Sarita, 'and I am glad he is dead. If I had the opportunity, I would have killed him myself. So what makes you think I will snitch?'

TWENTY-FOUR

Rastogi heard similar stories from the other two inmates he had shortlisted for interviews. The prisoners despised Deshmukh and his team, and if they knew something, they were not going to tell him. Yet, Deshmukh was a big, strong man, and Rastogi could not imagine a woman killing him. *But I have seen stranger things,* he thought. *Rage could have made it possible.*

He sat in Deshmukh's office, thinking of how to proceed. His thoughts were interrupted by a loud growl from his stomach. It was almost 3 p.m., he realised, and he had not eaten anything since the morning. He stepped out of the room, stretched and looked around for Kadam and Bapat. Then he started for the main gate, intending to have a quick lunch.

As he walked, he passed the prison canteen where

prisoners could buy essentials like soap, milk and oil with their own money. These provisions were supplied to the canteen by NGOs. Rastogi saw a group of inmates flocking to the small window of the canteen to make their meagre purchases. He knew that most of the things bought by the inmates would be taken away from them by the jail guards. The inmates knew this as well and could only hope that they got to use at least some of the items.

Rastogi had turned left at the corner of the canteen, when he saw a group of guards outside an adjacent room. Loud noises and cheers were audible, and as he came closer, he saw that it was full of jail officials. He stood behind the group near the open door and peeked inside. All eyes were glued on a 32-inch television mounted on the wall. An India-Pakistan cricket match was being telecast live.

Suddenly, he heard a collective sigh, followed by a flurry of expletives from the room. India's top batsman and team captain, Virat Kohli, had just been bowled. The group went into a detailed analysis of how Virat should have played the shot. Kadam and Bapat, deep in animated conversation, strolled out of the room. Only after they had passed Rastogi did Kadam spot him and turned back.

'Sir ... we just came here ... how were the meetings?' Kadam asked sheepishly.

Rastogi gave them both a disapproving look. His stomach growled again. 'Let's go for lunch,' he said.

TWENTY-FIVE

'So, I know everything that is happening here,' Rastogi said, looking at Bapat as he polished off the last spoonful of his chicken biryani.

'Well, I don't understand,' replied Bapat, still halfway through his meal.

'Let's cut to the chase, Bapat. There is no point denying what's been going on. But, if you help me, you may just be able to avoid Deshmukh's fate.'

Bapat stopped licking his oil-smeared fingers and stared at Rastogi. 'What do you mean … by that?'

'I mean that I am reasonably sure Deshmukh was murdered by a relative of one of the inmates, or an inmate who was released from the prison. They certainly had the motive to kill him, and the will too, apparently ... and Deshmukh's cronies could be next in line! So help me catch the killer.'

Bapat nodded vigorously.

'Good. Tell me, was there an inmate whom Deshmukh had singled out and was especially abusive towards?'

Bapat gulped, then said, 'There was one, Arti Shetye, for whom Deshmukh had a special liking ... over more than four years ... he violated her, almost every day ... it was brutal ... I tried to stop him on a couple of occasions, but ...'

'What happened to her?'

'She was acquitted around a year back. Good for her, she would not have survived much longer here. Of course, Deshmukh was disappointed at her release.'

'But from what you tell me, didn't Deshmukh try to locate her after her release?'

'He wanted to ... in fact, he had asked me to trace her whereabouts ... but a few days after that, the enquiry started, and he got busy with that. But, recently, he asked me about Arti again ... if I had managed to find out where she is.'

'And you have not been able to trace her.' Rastogi sighed and signalled to a waiter for the bill.

'Actually, I have. I just didn't tell Deshmukh.'

TWENTY-SIX

The Adarsh Nagar chawl is situated in the north Mumbai suburb of Kanjurmarg. A chawl is a type of residential building unique to Mumbai, especially the northern and central parts, constructed in the early 1900s to provide affordable housing to the city's mill-workers. Adarsh Nagar was one of the few remaining chawls in the area; many others had made way for high-rises, their extinction hastened by the closing of most of the mills.

The chawl consisted of three adjoining blocks in a huge 'C' formation. The central square, within the enclosed area, was the size of a quarter of a football field. Each block was three-storeyed, with twelve rooms on every floor, each measuring 150 square feet. A long, narrow passage ran the length of each floor, folding into a central staircase at the exact centre of each passage, with six rooms on either side. There was a common block of toilets on either side of the passage, which was shared by the families living on the floor. The doors to most rooms in the chawl were always open, with neighbours walking in and out of each other's homes freely and at all times.

It was 8 a.m., but the sun was obscured by ominously dark clouds that threatened to burst any time. The old woman, sensing the impending downpour, rushed to the terrace to gather the clothes she had hung out to dry overnight. She had just unclipped the last garment from the clothesline when she saw the younger woman, a solitary figure leaning on the parapet. She was heartbroken seeing her this way—alone, sad and angry. She had watched her grow up—a cheerful child, full of life. The old woman muttered a silent prayer for her, and setting her heap of clothes down by the entrance to the terrace, went up to her.

'Arti, how are you? I didn't see you the whole of last week. Where have you been?' The old woman stood next to her, her kind eyes smiling.

'Oh, I had gone to Pune,' Arti said softly, and then looked away.

'So you have made up your mind to go away?'

'Yes, I cannot take this city any longer,' Arti replied.

'I understand ... what will you do there? How will you stay alone?'

Arti read the concern in the old woman's question. And she knew how right she was. While she had been acquitted by law, her sentence continued in another sense. She now understood what *exclusion* meant. Her graduation meant nothing to prospective employers; the only qualification she seemed to possess in their eyes was the time she had served in prison. And this was the easy part. It was her thirteenth month out of Deshmukh's clutches, but the nightmares wouldn't stop. She still couldn't sleep at night. Would she ever get rid of him? Would a change of city help?

And what about him? Would she survive without his help?

TWENTY-SEVEN

'You are in early today,' Neel said, surprised to see Jaya come in before her usual time.

'Gaurav has gone out of town with his friends, so I didn't have too much to do in the morning.' Jaya smiled and continued, 'I don't see much of him these days.'

'What has he been up to?'

'Only He knows,' Jaya said, looking skywards and raising her hands. 'Comes in late almost every night. And he doesn't talk to me at all.'

'It's his age, Jaya. Let him be. Aren't you happy nagging only me?' Neel chuckled.

'No, I am serious. He was never like this; looks worried all the time these days.'

'Maybe he has a girlfriend?' Neel suggested.

'Maybe. Will you please talk to him and figure out what is bothering him?'

'Of course, Jaya. Don't worry,' Neel said reassuringly as he sat down on his chair and picked up the newspaper.

'Thank you. I have sorted your mail, and the day's schedule is here,' Jaya said, pointing to a sheet of printed paper.

'Um ... sorry, Jaya ... what was that?' Neel asked, his eyes fixed on an article on page two of *The Times of India*.

'Today's schedule is—' Jaya started, and then stopped herself. Neel was engrossed in the newspaper. She smiled, turned and quietly left his room.

TWENTY-EIGHT

Holding *The Times of India* tightly in his hands, the man strode up the floors from his room on the first. He reached the last room to the right and was disappointed to see the door was latched. Deciding to wait, he read the news article on the second page again. That is why he was there, to show her the article.

He was lost in his thoughts when, without warning, it started to pour. He shook his head in disappointment. He simply hated the rains. But he could not miss work. Not today. Today, he would have to go.

Five minutes later, he decided to walk back to his room, pick up his umbrella, and leave for office. As soon as he reached the staircase, he heard her voice. She was coming down, and she was not alone. He quickly retraced his steps towards her room and waited.

She was now on the same floor, politely listening to a woman clutching a heap of clothes to her chest. *Come on, you old hag, get lost.* He was losing his cool. Finally, he saw her wave a subdued goodbye to the old woman and start walking towards her room. Towards him. He smiled.

She was looking down, oblivious to his presence, as she reached her door. She unlatched it and was about to step in, when he called out, 'Arti, how are you?'

She turned around to see her neighbour from the first floor. She gave him a slight smile and was about to enter her room, when he said, 'There is something you must see.' He held the newspaper to his chest with one hand, tapping the article on page two with the other. She came forward and took the newspaper, her eyes fixed on the article.

She read it, her pretty face betraying no emotion. But when she finally looked up at him, her eyes were teary. 'Is this really true?'

'It is. He is dead, Arti. Ramakant Deshmukh is dead.'

Arti slumped forward, as if from exhaustion. He held her gently by the shoulders and led her inside her room. Then he brought her a glass of water from a clay pot, but she slowly shook her head, staring into empty space, still trying to digest the news. *He is dead. But is it over?*

'I will leave now. You take care ... and let me know if you need any help,' the man said.

Arti nodded.

It was still raining when he left Arti's room. He cursed under his breath; he could not miss office that day. Manohar Rao walked to his first-floor room, picked up his umbrella and left for the clinic. He had to take care of important business that day—it was a matter of life and death.

Despite the rains, he could not stop smiling as he reached the station. *Maybe she will relent now. If this didn't help, he did not know what else would.*

TWENTY-NINE

'Wait for me here,' Rastogi told Kadam, two hundred metres from the entrance to the Adarsh Nagar chawl. Kadam, not one to question his boss, parked the police car immediately. It was after 11 a.m., and the rains continued unabated. Rastogi leaned out of the car, opened his umbrella and with a grunt, lifted his heavy frame out. He carefully avoided the puddles as he walked towards the chawl. Small shops and kiosks lined the narrow lane, makeshift plastic shutters drawn down to keep the merchandise safe from the rains. Rastogi smelled samosas as he passed an eatery, and smiled to himself. It was ideal weather for samosas. *Much less ideal circumstances*, he quickly reminded himself.

He was dressed in a plain half-sleeved shirt and trousers, having changed out of his uniform before leaving the station. He had seen the surprise on Kadam's face when he had asked him to stop quite a distance away from their destination. Rastogi empathised with Arti's situation—acquittal after years of wrongful imprisonment, the trauma of Deshmukh's abuse, and probably the worst of all, the social ostracism faced by all ex-prisoners. He did not want to add to her misery by taking a police car to her front door.

Bapat had given him the complete address, so he did not need to ask for directions. He looked at the central staircase winding steeply up the tenement and swore. There were very few occasions when Rastogi lamented his complete lack of interest in keeping fit, and this was one of those. He counted the twelve steps between each floor, resting for a few seconds to catch his breath when he reached the landings. Finally, he stopped to wipe the sweat off his brow on the third floor. *I just hope she is at home,* he said to himself as he walked towards Arti's room at the far end.

THIRTY

Arti was reading the newspaper article for the umpteenth time, as if to reconfirm the death of her tormentor again and again. Her initial shock at hearing the news had turned into relief, and hope. She also felt a deep sense of gratitude towards Manohar. Had he not extended his help at the right time, she may not have survived. It was very obvious how he felt about her. *Someday, maybe I will be ready to feel the same way,* she thought.

Just then, another thought struck her, and she froze in a disbelief that bordered on horror. *Manohar.* She had witnessed him lose his temper a few times, and knew about his time in juvenile prison. *Had he repeated his crime? Killed for her, like he had for his mother?*

Her thoughts were interrupted by a knock on her already open door. She turned to see a plump, short man, who walked in before she could say anything.

THIRTY-ONE

'Arti Shetye?'
'Yes ... but ... who are you?'
'I am Inspector Abhay Rastogi, Crime Branch. I am investigating the murder of Ramakant Deshmukh.'

A sudden panic hit Arti, the blood draining from her face so fast she had to sit down. Rastogi sat on the only chair available in the room, facing Arti, who was seated on her single bed. He glanced at the newspaper beside her; he had read the article that morning.

'I know what he did to you ... I know it all ... but even if he was a monster, he was murdered. And I intend to find out who did it,' Rastogi said.

'I ... I don't know anything about it ... in fact, I just came to know about his death,' Arti said, pointing to the newspaper, open at the page with the report on Deshmukh's murder.

Rastogi looked at the frail, pretty woman in front of him. He knew she was in her early thirties, but she looked a few years older, thin and tired. Yet attractive. *There was no way she could have taken out Deshmukh. But then, he was drunk, and she, filled with rage. Maybe she had help.*

'Tell me about your family, Arti. Where are they?'

Arti shook her head. 'My parents died when I was fifteen. Since then, I have been alone.'

'And you have stayed here all along?'

'Yes, except for the time I was in…'

'Yes, of course, I understand,' Rastogi said, shrugging his shoulders. He wanted to avoid talking about what he already knew and it probably didn't matter to the case. He knew she had been imprisoned for murdering her husband. She had pleaded her innocence all along and was acquitted after a protracted legal battle.

'And what do you do for a living?' he asked.

'I was working as a medical nurse in a private hospital before …' Arti hesitated. Rastogi nodded, urging her to continue.

'After I was released,' Arti looked down, 'I could not find employment for a couple of months. But later, with the help of a friend, I got a job at the Bombay Government Hospital.'

THIRTY-TWO

Rastogi made an entry in his black diary and asked, 'Where were you the night Deshmukh was killed?'

'I was in Pune the whole of last week, and returned yesterday at around 5 p.m.,' she said.

'Why did you go to Pune?'

'I have been looking for a change of place ... after what ... happened here ...' her voice trailed off. She sighed and continued, 'I went there looking for work, visited a few hospitals, but...'

Rastogi noted down the names of the hospitals Arti said she had visited. He would have that checked.

'You wanted to leave Mumbai because you were scared that Deshmukh might find you?'

Arti nodded, shivering slightly.

'And now that he is dead?'

'I don't know … maybe … maybe not.'

Holding on to his knees, Rastogi slowly got up. Arti stood up too, looking relieved.

'One last question … for now,' Rastogi said. 'What is the name of your friend, the one who helped you get the job here?'

'Manohar Rao, he stays on the first floor.'

THIRTY-THREE

The rains had subsided and Kadam was sipping a chai, leaning against the car, when he saw Rastogi walking back towards him. From his stride, he could make out that his boss was on to something. It was his sixth year working with Rastogi, and his respect for him had only grown over the years. He ordered another chai and handed it to Rastogi.

'Ah, just what I needed,' Rastogi said, raising the short glass in appreciation.

'So, what is our next move?' Kadam asked.

Rastogi swallowed the hot, milky liquid in one big slurp, handed the glass and ten rupees to the vendor, and gestured to Kadam to start driving. Over the next ten minutes, Rastogi filled Kadam in on the details of his conversation with Arti.

'His room was locked, so I am going to visit the clinic he works at,' Rastogi said, reading the entry in his black diary. 'Dr Neel Burman ... head towards Peddar Road.'

Kadam eased the police car on to the Eastern Express Highway, expecting to cover the thirty kilometres to their destination in about an hour. It was just after noon and the highway was clogged with traffic. Kadam frowned and looked at Rastogi, who was sitting with his eyes closed, deep in thought.

'I have a question,' Kadam said as they were waiting at a red light. Rastogi opened his eyes, as if a switch had been turned on, and looked at Kadam. The lights turned green and Kadam put the car in gear.

'We have a clear lead for Deshmukh's murder: Deshmukh to Arti to Manohar. Worth investigating. But how is Alok Dalal linked to all of this?'

Rastogi smiled approvingly. He had expected—in fact, was waiting for—this question from Kadam.

'So, there are three possibilities,' Rastogi said, and paused dramatically, as he liked doing. 'One, we are barking up the wrong tree: Arti or Manohar may have nothing to do with Deshmukh's murder. If that is the case, we are back to square one.'

Kadam nodded.

'Two,' Rastogi continued, 'The two murders are completely unrelated.' Kadam looked sharply at his boss but before he could protest, Rastogi said, 'I know, I know ... the modus operandi is the same in both the murders ... the rod, and especially the post-it notes. But it could be a copy-cat killer.'

'And three, the two cases are linked—we just haven't figured out how.' Rastogi concluded.

'So, what are we going to do?' Kadam asked.

'I want you to do something,' Rastogi replied.

THIRTY-FOUR

Charu got out of the Uber and walked into the compound of the building where Neel had his clinic. The fickle Mumbai weather was at its worst—or best—as the heavy showers of the morning had given way to a bright day. Charu's yellow dress mirrored her sunny mood; her new book was going into production. She had planned a celebratory lunch with Neel.

She warmly greeted the watchman and headed for the elevator. Just as she pressed '3' and the doors were closing, Manohar stepped in, looked at Charu and greeted her, 'Good afternoon, Madam.'

'How are you, Manohar?' Charu asked, forcing a smile. She had never really liked Manohar. She looked at her phone, as the old elevator slowly inched up the three storeys. But she could sense Manohar's gaze on her, and she flushed. As the doors opened on the third floor, she was moving out, eyes fixed on her phone, when Manohar brushed against her, also trying to step out of the elevator. Startled, Charu dropped her phone and glared at Manohar. 'Idiot,' she muttered under her breath, but loud enough for Manohar to hear. He just stared at her and mumbled an apology as she picked up her phone and stormed away.

THIRTY-FIVE

Charu entered the clinic and sat in the reception area, still fuming. Jaya wasn't at her seat, although she could see her handbag on the front desk. The main door to the clinic opened and Manohar stepped in. He stopped briefly in front of Charu, but just then, Jaya came out of the connecting door to the waiting room. Manohar walked to his desk, took a few files out of the drawer and disappeared into the adjoining passage.

'Hi Charu, how are you?' Jaya exclaimed and walked towards her, arms wide open. Charu smiled and stood up; the two women exchanged a warm hug.

'How are you, Jaya? Hope your boss is treating you well?' Charu laughed. She was very fond of Jaya and admired her for the lady she was.

'He is the best! In fact, he is talking to Gaurav at the moment,' Jaya said, pointing to Neel's door. Charu had met Gaurav on a few occasions, and she knew how fond Neel was of the young man.

'Oh, really! It will be great to meet him,' she said.

'I will tell him you are here, please have a seat' said Jaya, and walked towards Neel's cabin. Charu turned around and caught Manohar staring at her. She sat down, hoping Neel would come out soon and they could leave.

In another five minutes, Neel came out of his cabin, accompanied by a young man in a white shirt and denims, sporting a trendy hairstyle and a beard. He bore a striking resemblance to Jaya, who was all smiles as she followed them out of the cabin. While Charu walked over to the trio, Manohar, who was poring over some papers at his desk, did not move from his seat.

'Hello, Charu Ma'am. How are you?' Gaurav smiled at her.

'Hi Gaurav, so nice to see you. How have you been?' Charu asked.

'I am doing great, Ma'am.'

'Gaurav has decided to do his post-graduation,' Neel chipped in.

'Oh, that's great!' Charu said.

'All thanks to sir,' Gaurav said, looking gratefully at Neel, who gave him an encouraging pat on his back.

'Shall we go?' Neel smiled at Charu.

THIRTY-SIX

'You seem upset about something,' said Neel, as he started the car.

Charu sighed. 'It's Manohar,' she said and narrated the elevator incident. 'He is disgusting … and don't try to defend him this time.'

They drove in silence for a few minutes.

'I have told you before that you made a mistake giving him this job. He is a criminal for God's sake!'

'He has paid the price for it, Charu.'

'A few years in a juvenile home? That's the price for killing someone?'

'But that's the law, Charu. And I am sure he is a reformed man now.'

'Crime is a habit, Neel.'

THIRTY-SEVEN

'I can see a very positive change in you.' Neel smiled at his patient.

'Yes, I am feeling much better. It's as though all the demons have been killed,' she said.

'And are you able to sleep now?'

'Like a baby,' she laughed.

'That's great. I am so happy to hear that. I think you can stop the medication completely, starting today.'

'Are you sure, doctor? I mean, I have been taking the pills for four years now.'

'Positive. Stop immediately. You don't need them anymore; in fact, you don't need these sessions either,' Neel said, smiling affectionately at his young patient.

'Oh, that's sad … I kind of liked coming here.' She made a mock long face.

'Come,' said Neel, and he gently led her out of his cabin into the waiting room. The woman seated there looked up at the sound of the door opening, put a magazine back on the centre table, and smiled at Neel.

'Good to see you, Mrs Dalal. Your daughter is absolutely fine now,' Neel said.

Madhoo Dalal beamed and hugged Nitya.

THIRTY-EIGHT

The mother-daughter duo came out of the building, laughing and talking animatedly, and walked to the main road. They got into their chauffeur-driven Toyota Camry, and drove away into the evening traffic. Once the car was out of sight, Kadam emerged from the building across the street where he had been waiting, under instructions from his boss to keep an eye on Nitya. Whether Rastogi had a solid theory or it was just a shot in the dark, he did not know, but on the third day of following Nitya Dalal, he had just hit on a lead that might crack the case.

Arti's friend worked at the clinic of Nitya's doctor. *Manohar Rao, you are the common link to the two cases*, Kadam smiled to himself. Then he dialled Rastogi's number.

THIRTY-NINE

At 11 a.m. on the following day, Rastogi and Kadam visited Neel's clinic. Seeing two men in police uniforms, Jaya was startled; thankful, too, that there were no patients in the clinic.

'How can I help you, Inspector?' Jaya asked, looking at Rastogi, and then at Kadam.

'Does Manohar Rao work here?' It was Kadam who asked. Rastogi was admiring the tastefully decorated clinic.

'Yes, he does. Is there a problem?'

'Where is he?' Kadam inquired. Rastogi, leaning forward, hands behind his back, was now looking at the various certificates on display on the reception's walls.

'He is not in ... hasn't come for the last three days ... but, has anything happened, Inspector?'

'Hmm,' Rastogi nodded thoughtfully and continued, 'is Dr Burman in?' He had completed his short tour of the reception.

'Yes, he is,' Jaya said, and getting up, led them to Neel's cabin. She knocked softly, twice, as she normally did.

'Come in, Jaya,' Neel said, typing on his laptop with his reading glasses on. He saw the two policemen on Jaya's heels, and took his glasses off. 'Yes?' he asked.

'Dr Burman, sorry to come unannounced.' Rastogi said, not looking sorry at all. Neel gestured to the sofa in the corner of his cabin. As the men shook hands and exchanged introductions, Jaya left the room.

'So, how can I help you, Inspector Rastogi?' Neel asked once they had settled on the sofa.

'There have been two unfortunate incidents, doctor.' Rastogi gave Neel a brief update about the two murders and the progress the police had made on the cases. 'And our investigation has led us to one of your employees, Manohar Rao,' Rastogi concluded.

'Manohar? You think he has committed the murders? I can't believe that!'

'We will find out, doctor. As of now, we need to talk to him.'

'I don't think he has come to work for a couple of days. But I can give you his address,' Neel offered.

'We already know where he lives, thank you. Can you tell us something more about Manohar?'

'Well, it was around twelve years ago that I first met him. An NGO, which works for the rehabilitation of juvenile convicts approached the hospital, urging us to employ some of them. Manohar was one of them, and he has worked for me ever since.'

'And how has his behaviour been—on the job?'

'Manohar could have done much better, but he is quite lazy and unambitious ... erratic ... irregular.'

'Has he been clean since his release?' Rastogi asked, leaning forward.

'I ... I think so, Inspector ... let's say he makes people uncomfortable ... but no major troubles,' Neel said.

'Uncomfortable, you say?'

Neel described the recent incident with Charu and Jaya's instincts about Manohar. Rastogi made notes in his diary.

'Why was Manohar in the juvenile home?' Rastogi asked, looking at Neel.

Neel looked at Rastogi, pursed his lips, and said, 'He had killed a man ... his neighbour ... in a fit of rage.'

FORTY

'That was good work, Kadam,' Rastogi said. 'This is the breakthrough we needed.'

Kadam acknowledged the compliment with a wide grin. It was rare, coming from Rastogi. 'Do we go to Adarsh Nagar now?'

Rastogi looked at his watch, an old HMT. It was past noon. He shook his head. 'We won't find him there at this time. Let's go and say hello to Madhoo Dalal.'

They got into the police car and took a right turn, heading south towards the Dalal residence.

From behind the curtain of a window in the clinic, Jaya Shetty stood looking at the police car until it climbed over the Kemps Corner flyover and disappeared from view.

FORTY-ONE

Across the road from Neel's clinic was an Irani restaurant, a favourite with the locals and tourists alike. Over the last few years, scenes for many Bollywood movies had been shot there, increasing its popularity. Seated at his regular spot in the restaurant, Manohar finished his late breakfast—a double-omelette with pav, followed by an Irani chai. Then he crossed the congested main road, swearing at a biker who whizzed past, and entered the compound of the clinic. He froze.

Two policemen were talking to the security guard. One was short and fat, more likely the senior officer, and the other was tall and lanky. Manohar hid behind a parked car, but could overhear them asking for directions to Dr Burman's clinic. He turned, walking as casually as he could until he turned right on the main road, where he hastened his pace, soon breaking into a run.

How could they have known?

FORTY-TWO

'Good afternoon, Mrs Dalal,' Rastogi bowed a little and smiled when Madhoo answered the door.

'Oh, hello Inspector.' Madhoo seemed taken aback at seeing the cops.

Without waiting for an invitation, Rastogi and Kadam walked in and sat down in the living room. Madhoo joined them; she appeared fidgety. Before Rastogi could start, she called out to the maid and asked her to get two cups of tea.

'Any development on the case?' Madhoo asked.

'There are a couple of angles we are looking at. I am sure we will nab the killer very soon.'

'I hope so ... how can I help you, Inspector?'

'Is your daughter at home?'

Madhoo suddenly went pale. 'No ... she is not ... she has gone out ... but why are you asking?'

'Oh, it's nothing, Mrs Dalal. Tell us, do you know someone called Manohar Rao?'

'Umm ... Manohar Rao ... no, the name is not familiar.'

'Are you sure? Think carefully,' Rastogi insisted.

'Should I know him?'

'You haven't met him at Dr Burman's clinic?' asked Rastogi, narrowing his eyes.

'Dr Burman ... how did you ... oh yes, there is a Manohar at his clinic ... but I didn't recollect it offhand.'

'No problem. Now that you remember, did you or Nitya interact with him much?'

'No ... maybe briefly, once or twice. But mostly it was his receptionist, Jaya, with whom we spoke when we called to make appointments.'

'And why does Nitya consult Dr Burman?'

FORTY-THREE

Madhoo was silent for a minute. Just then the maid came in, carrying a tray with cups of tea, glasses of water and a plate of assorted biscuits. Madhoo dismissed her with a swift wave of her hand.

'What does that have to do with the case?' she asked in a firm tone that Rastogi had not associated with her personality until then.

'Maybe nothing. But maybe it could help us solve the case.' Rastogi sipped his tea, trying to sound as casual as he could. Kadam was on his third biscuit.

Madhoo sat there, saying nothing, motionless.

'Look, Mrs Dalal, we will get this information anyway—*all* the details—once we go with a warrant to Dr Burman. But if that happens, many others will hear about it. The judicial process will expose the details of your private life to many eyes, and there are very high chances that our findings will also be leaked to the media.' Rastogi spoke calmly. He could see that Madhoo was making a decision, so he continued, 'Here we can keep it between us, I promise.'

Madhoo exhaled and got up. 'Come with me,' she said and led them to the bedroom at the far end of the corridor off the living room. She closed the door once Rastogi and Kadam were inside.

She opened her mouth to speak, but stopped herself, as if trying to choose the right words. 'So,' she finally said, 'Nitya has been seeing Dr Burman for the past four years, since she was fifteen. She was a complete mess, until—'

Madhoo stopped abruptly. Rastogi waited for her to compose herself.

'Nitya is not Alok's daughter,' Madhoo announced suddenly and looked at the floor. Rastogi kept his eyes fixed on Madhoo, not betraying his reaction. Kadam let out a little gasp.

'I married Alok when Nitya was eight. Initially, I thought nothing of it ... just a new stepfather trying hard to bond with his stepdaughter. But soon, Nitya started avoiding Alok; she seemed to want to be around me all the time. I rationalised the situation—it was a new home, new beginnings—so she wanted to stay close to me and wasn't comfortable being alone with Alok. But the other things that I remember so vividly now, I wonder how I could have missed them then. The despair in her eyes, her silent complaints ...' Madhoo said softly as tears welled up in her eyes.

She sniffed, wiped her tears, and continued, 'Nitya became increasingly withdrawn as the ... the abuse continued ... sometimes by manipulation, sometimes by coercion. She stopped sleeping, fearing he might come into her room at night. Alok became more and more brazen as the years went by, but successfully maintained his clean, family-man image in public.'

Rastogi came across instances of child sexual abuse very frequently in his line of work. Yet, none of these cases had rattled him as much as Nitya's story. *The most heinous of crimes often go unreported*, he reflected.

'And why did *you* not take any action?' he asked.

'Initially, it was disbelief. Maybe, I did not want to believe ... I was so blinded by my love for Alok ... and then, the shame. I felt so ... powerless ...' Her voice trailed off.

'And Nitya? How did she take this ... your inaction?'

'I know I have failed her ... I could understand her anger towards me. After all, I had failed to protect her. But over time, she probably realised my helpless situation and her bitterness towards me softened. At least, outwardly it has.'

'So that explains Dr Burman,' Rastogi said.

Madhoo nodded. 'I took Nitya to Dr Burman after her condition deteriorated, and she started to have anxiety attacks. His counselling and medications helped calm her down.'

'And after Alok died?'

'Nitya is a changed person, miraculously. In fact, Dr Burman said she does not need therapy or medicines anymore,' Madhoo said, smiling through her tears.

'And now, Mrs Dalal, can you tell us anything more about your husband's murder?'

FORTY-FOUR

Madhoo looked at Rastogi, stunned. 'What are you trying to say? That I had a hand in my husband's murder?'

'No, no, Mrs Dalal, you misunderstand me. But there has been another murder, similar to how Mr Dalal was killed. And we are following up on a lead that involves Manohar Rao at Dr Burman's clinic. So, it's important that you tell us how well you or Nitya know Manohar.'

Madhoo shook her head, deep creases on her forehead. 'No, as I said earlier, we have rarely interacted with Manohar—that too, the way one would with a receptionist. That's all I can tell you, sorry.'

'Is it likely that Nitya knows him any better?'

'No, I am quite sure she doesn't. She is not very outgoing anyway, has very few friends, so ... I would say, unlikely ... no, in fact, it's impossible.'

'A final request, Mrs Dalal, before we leave,' Rastogi said.

'Sure, Inspector.'

'Can we have another cup of tea?'

Madhoo smiled for the first time that afternoon.

FORTY-FIVE

The lights turned red, and the vehicles on the busy road came to a halt. A sea of office-goers surged in both directions to cross the main street, eager to reach home. One person, however, stood frozen at the end of the pedestrian crossing until jostled by the crowd. Still lost in thought, the killer hurried towards the pavement as the lights turned green.

How did the police come to know? Was the game up? It couldn't be. I won't let it happen.

And then, plain as daylight, the killer knew what had to be done.

FORTY-SIX

The Bombay Government Hospital, founded in the early 1900s, is located in the central suburb of Parel in Mumbai. With more than 500 resident doctors and 2,200 beds, it is one of the biggest hospitals in the city. Funded chiefly by the city's municipal corporation, it was also the hospital of choice for the underprivileged, as it offered free medical services to the poor.

However, the hospital was struggling to manage the increasing number of patients. Its infrastructure was in a shambles. A month back, it made headlines when it ran out of water for three days, including the supply that was reserved for emergencies. Even surgeries had to be cancelled until water tankers arrived on the third day.

A BRUTAL HAND

Arti checked on the last patient on her roster for the afternoon, and then returned to the staff room. She picked up her lunch box, crossed the corridor and took the stairs to the staff cafeteria, one level above. Taking a clean plate and a spoon from the counter, she sat down at a corner table and opened her box.

Just then, her phone rang.

'Hello, Manohar,' she said.

'Listen, Arti, I am going out of town for a few days. Do not worry about me. And if anyone comes asking about me, tell them you do not know anything.'

'You've got me worried. Is everything okay?'

The line was so silent that Arti checked her phone to see if the call had dropped.

'Manohar, are you there?'

'Don't worry, take care of yourself,' he said, and disconnected the call.

Arti sighed and shook her head. She whispered a silent prayer; she knew he was in trouble. *Will I see you again, Manohar?*

FORTY-SEVEN

'So, it's all done. We start next month,' Kunal Roy, the CEO of Words & More Publications, told Charu.

'Sounds great, looking forward to the chaos,' Charu laughed, looking once again at her book launch itinerary, which covered twenty-six events in two months.

Charu picked up her handbag, bade Kunal goodbye, and left his swanky twentieth-floor office in Nariman Point. She looked at her phone for the first time in two hours as she got into the elevator and pressed P2, where her car was parked. There were three messages from Neel, the last one at 10.50 p.m., which was twenty minutes ago. *He must be worried sick,* she thought.

'Sorry, just finished. Leaving now. See you in twenty,' she messaged Neel on Whatsapp. The two ticks turned blue immediately.

'Great, see you soon,' came the reply.

FORTY-EIGHT

Charu got into the driver's seat of her Jeep Compass in the deserted basement parking podium. She put her handbag and phone next to her on the passenger seat and adjusted the rearview mirror. She was about to start the car when her phone buzzed. She saw Kunal's name flashing on the screen.

Before Charu could pick it up, the vibrating phone fell off the edge of the seat. Charu cursed, unfastened her seat belt, and bent down to pick up the phone. At that very moment, an iron rod crashed into the steering wheel, missing her head by mere inches.

Charu screamed as she turned around to see the masked assailant, in a black trench coat and a hoodie, raise the rod once again for a second strike. Charu jumped clumsily over to the passenger side, opened the door and tried to scramble out. The rod came down once again, and this time it did not miss.

FORTY-NINE

Charu screamed in pain as the rod smashed into her left calf while she was throwing herself out of the car. She fell out awkwardly, clutching her leg. Seeing her attacker open the rear door, she got up, grimacing as she put pressure on her injured leg, and limped as fast as she could towards the lift lobby.

'Help me,' she screamed. She could hear the assailant's feet thumping behind her, and expected a second blow any moment now. She realised she was weeping.

One of the six elevators chimed, with a bright yellow arrow pointing upwards, and Kunal walked out.

'Help!' Charu howled again, then fainted. In the moment before darkness engulfed her, she could see a hazy figure running towards her.

FIFTY

'He must have stayed over somewhere,' Kadam said, suppressing a yawn. It was almost 1 a.m., and he was at the wheel of his police car, parked in the lane opposite the Adarsh Nagar chawl. Rastogi was seated beside him, his eyes glued to the entrance of the building. Earlier that night, Rastogi had gone up to Manohar's room, and upon finding it locked, decided to wait for him. They had been waiting for more than four hours.

Rastogi did not say anything. He was inclined to wait it out. He raised his hand, gesturing to Kadam to be patient. Kadam sighed and rolled his eyes when Rastogi was not looking.

Just then, Rastogi's three-year-old Samsung phone beeped.

'Dr Burman, is everything okay?' Rastogi asked, sounding worried.

'Charu has been attacked. We are at the Breach Candy hospital,' Neel said.

FIFTY-ONE

The resident doctor had just finished plastering Charu's leg when Rastogi and Kadam arrived at the hospital. Neel was with her, standing next to another man whom the policemen had not met.

'Don't worry, it's not a fracture. You can go home tomorrow, or maybe the day after.' The doctor smiled reassuringly.

'Thank God,' Neel said, kissing Charu's forehead. She smiled weakly at Rastogi and Kadam.

'I heard about the attack, Mrs Burman. You must consider yourself very lucky. By the way, I am Inspector Rastogi,' he smiled at Charu, 'and this is my colleague, Kadam.' Kadam greeted Charu with a smile.

'Inspector, this is Charu's publisher, Kunal Roy. He is the one who brought her here; in fact, he saved her life. If he had not been there at the right moment, I don't know what—' Neel broke off and patted Kunal on the shoulder.

Rastogi acknowledged the bespectacled middle-aged man with a nod. 'Haven't we met somewhere before?' Rastogi asked Kunal.

'No, Inspector, I am quite sure we are meeting for the first time,' Kunal said, looking surprised.

'You might have seen him on TV. Our man is a regular on the political news debates,' Neel said.

'Ah, then that's it,' Rastogi said. Looking at Charu, he asked, 'Are you in a position to discuss the unfortunate incident, Mrs Burman? I would not have bothered you so soon after the attack, but every minute is precious.'

'But …' Neel meekly protested.

'Sure, I am fine. Go ahead, Inspector.' Charu smiled at Neel, holding his hand.

Over the next ten minutes, Charu narrated the entire incident to Rastogi, from the time she left Kunal's office till the moment she lost consciousness.

'Hmm,' Rastogi said, making entries in his black book. 'Anything that can help us identify the attacker?'

'Nothing, sorry. He was completely covered in a black coat and a hoodie … plus a mask … so,' Charu shook her head.

'How do you know it was a *he*, Mrs Burman?'

'Pardon me?'

'I mean, you just said, "*He* was completely covered"?'

'Oh, I presumed it was a "*He*",' Charu said, shrugging her shoulders.

'But there must have been something which made you say that?'

'Actually, now that you mention it, no. It could have been a woman as well.'

FIFTY-TWO

'Can you tell us what happened, Mr Roy?' Rastogi asked, looking at Kunal.

'After Charu left my office, I called her to clarify a certain point we were discussing. She did not answer. But that could have waited, so I wound up my work and left. And as soon as I stepped out of the lift, I saw Charu screaming. By the time I reached her, she had fainted. So, I brought her to the hospital, and on the way, I informed Neel.'

'And did you see anyone pursuing her? The masked assailant?'

'Nope, I did not see anyone,' Kunal said, shaking his head.

Must be hiding somewhere, inferred Rastogi.

FIFTY-THREE

'Thank you, Mrs Burman,' Rastogi said, bowing a little to Charu. 'If you recollect anything else, please let us know.'

'Kadam, you go with Mr Roy to where Mrs Burman's car is parked,' Rastogi said. 'See if you find something. I hope you don't mind, Mr Roy?'

'Sure, no problem at all,' Kunal said. Kadam nodded, and the two men left. Neel walked Rastogi out of the room.

'Don't worry, Dr Burman, everything will be alright,' Rastogi said, perceiving Neel's agitation.

'Why would Manohar want to attack Charu? I just don't get it,' Neel said.

'There are two assumptions here, Dr Burman,' Rastogi said, mildly admonishing. 'First, that this attacker *is* the killer we are looking for ... and two, supposing it is indeed the same person, that that person is Manohar.'

'Yeah, you are right. I just jumped to conclusions ... sorry,' Neel said sheepishly, before continuing, 'but, I cannot help it ... the murderer is still out there ... and Charu and Inaaya—'

'I understand your concerns. Restrict your family's movements, including yours, for some time. Don't let your daughter go out alone in the evenings. Mrs Burman,' Rastogi said, glancing at Charu inside the room, 'will be indisposed for a few days in any case.'

'Sure, I will do that,' Neel agreed.

Rastogi left the hospital and took a taxi home. He was eager to hear from Kadam.

FIFTY-FOUR

Rastogi stepped into his one-bedroom flat at 2 a.m. Famished, he opened the refrigerator, hoping to find some leftovers, although he thought it unlikely. He was right; the fridge was empty, except for two bottles of water and an empty egg-tray. He sighed, took out a bottle of water, and switching on the television, sat down on the sofa. The living room was sparsely furnished, with a lone two-seater sofa, a wooden centre table and two rickety chairs. He drank half the bottle in a few gulps, opened his black diary, and read through his notes on the case. Turning the last written page, he closed his eyes and reflected, shaking and nodding his head from time to time.

He had listed Alok Dalal and Ramakant Deshmukh

as victims on these pages. He corrected the nomenclature in his head.

They were both killed, and hence, were victims in a certain sense. But the real victims were Nitya and Arti.

His thoughts were interrupted by the ringing of his phone. Replacing the bottle on the centre table, he answered the call, 'Yes, Kadam.'

'Sir, it's the same killer,' Kadam said. 'Mrs Burman is lucky to be alive.'

'And how do you know it's the same killer?'

'I found a post-it note below the rear seat of the car. It must have fallen during the scuffle.'

'And the post-it has ...'

'Yes, sir, it has "*Sorry*" written on it,' Kadam said, before Rastogi could complete his sentence.

Rastogi hung up, made some more notes in his diary, and went back to his contemplation. As soon as he closed his eyes, exhaustion overpowered him and he fell asleep, but not before he had chalked out his next plan of action.

FIFTY-FIVE

The next morning, Rastogi and Kadam returned to Adarsh Nagar. This time, Kadam parked the car in the chawl's central square, at the entrance to the block where Manohar stayed. The police car invited quite a few curious looks from early morning office-goers, children off to school in a bright yellow van and the elderly folk chatting in the passages.

Rastogi and Kadam went straight to Manohar's room on the first floor but found it locked again. They made enquiries in the two next-door rooms, but nobody had seen Manohar during the past few days. Rastogi nodded to Kadam, and they went down the staircase. With numerous eyes on them, they got into their car and left. Kadam drove for around two hundred metres and stopped. He made the call, as instructed by Rastogi.

Ten minutes later, Arti walked up to the car. She was dressed in a saree, a handbag on her shoulder. Visibly perturbed, she looked around nervously, quickly opened the door and got into the car. Kadam eased the vehicle out towards the Bombay Government Hospital.

'Thank you,' Arti said. She meant it; she was just settling into a new life, and it would have made things even more difficult for her had the police come to her door.

'Do you know where Manohar is?' Rastogi asked, coming straight to the point.

He really is in trouble, Arti thought. *What have you done, Manohar?* She lied, 'No, I don't. I haven't seen him or spoken to him for the past few days. Is something wrong?'

'The matter is serious, Arti. We need to speak with him in connection with two murders and one attempt-to-murder.'

Arti froze. She had always had a hunch that Manohar was involved in Deshmukh's murder. 'I don't believe it. Manohar would never do anything like that,' she lied again.

'We will know in time,' Rastogi said calmly.

They drove in silence for the next fifteen minutes. Traffic was easy on the Eastern Freeway that morning, and as they were nearing the hospital, Rastogi asked Arti, 'Tell me, did you undergo any sort of therapy or counselling to overcome your trauma?'

'I ... yes, I did,' Arti said.

'And was it Manohar who suggested therapy?'

'Yes, he did. He said it would help, and it did.'

'And who was your counsellor?'

'Dr Neel Burman.'

FIFTY-SIX

They dropped Arti at the Bombay Government Hospital and headed towards Breach Candy hospital. Kadam looked questioningly at Rastogi, who gave him a smug smile.

'How did you know?' Kadam asked.

'A calculated guess,' Rastogi explained. 'Arti knows Manohar, who she claims is a good friend. She works at the Bombay Government Hospital, where Dr Burman consults. It is not difficult to imagine that Manohar could have recommended therapy with his employer to help overcome her trauma. Dr Burman is known to be the charitable sort, offering free psychiatric treatment at the hospital.'

'But how did you know that Dr. Burman practises

at the Bombay Government Hospital? He did not tell us that.'

'It was right in front of our eyes, my dear Kadam—the certificates on the wall in Dr Burman's reception.'

FIFTY-SEVEN

'Hello, Dr Burman. How is Mrs Burman feeling now?' Rastogi asked Neel as they sat in the cafeteria at the Breach Candy hospital. Neel looked haggard, dark circles under his eyes.

'Charu is sleeping; the doctor gave her a sleeping pill. Hopefully, she will be discharged in the evening,' he said, stifling a yawn.

'You should rest yourself, Dr Burman.'

'I am so worried. Are you any closer to nabbing Mano ... I mean, the suspect?'

'We are getting closer,' Rastogi said. 'Tell me, do you remember a patient named Arti Shetye?'

'Arti Shetye? Cannot recall immediately ... but I can look at my records, if it's important,' Neel offered.

'That will be very useful, Dr Burman. I would also like to look at Nitya Dalal's file. See if we can get a lead.'

'We can head to my clinic right away if you'd like. Inaaya is with Charu if she needs something.'

They quickly finished their cups of tea, and Neel informed Inaaya that he needed to make a short trip to the clinic. The three men headed towards the main exit of the hospital. Just as they were leaving, Gaurav walked in. Seeing Neel, the young man came up to him.

'Mom called me ... is Ma'am better now?' Gaurav asked.

'Yes ... um ... I will be back in some time, Gaurav,' Neel said absently, as he walked out of the building.

'Sure. I will be with Ma'am until then,' Gaurav said and approached the front desk.

FIFTY-EIGHT

Neel and Rastogi drove to the clinic in the doctor's car, Kadam following them in the police car. They covered the short distance in less than ten minutes.

Jaya had just cancelled the last of the day's appointments when they walked in. She looked at Neel, concern on her face. 'Is she better now?'

'Yes, Jaya, thanks. Anything important?'

'Nothing more important than what's going on with Charu,' she said.

'We would like to look at the patient files,' Rastogi said to Jaya, who looked at Neel. The doctor nodded.

'I will have a look, sir,' Kadam said.

Jaya led Kadam to the passage adjoining the reception area, where the storage cabinets were. The six cabinets, with two shelves each, were alphabetically labelled and neatly organised. Kadam knew exactly which files he wanted and opened the first cabinet.

Expecting Kadam to retrieve the files in a few minutes, Rastogi declined Neel's invitation to sit in his cabin and remained standing in the reception area. Neel waited with him. They could hear the sound of files being moved, paper rustling and cabinet doors being opened and shut as Kadam went about his business.

After about fifteen minutes, Rastogi sat down on the sofa in the reception area; Neel joined him. It was an hour before Kadam reappeared, his body damp with perspiration.

'Both the files are missing,' he announced.

FIFTY-NINE

'How is it possible? All my records are stored there!'
'Could you have put these files elsewhere, doctor?' Rastogi asked.

'No, no ... *all* my files should be there,' Neel said, throwing up his hands in frustration. Jaya, who was standing next to Kadam, nodded in agreement.

'Who has access to these shelves?'

'Well, Jaya has a set of keys; Manohar has another. But maintaining the files was Manohar's job.'

'I don't even remember the last time I opened those cabinets,' Jaya added.

'So along with Manohar, the files are also missing,' Rastogi declared.

SIXTY

Two weeks had passed since the attack on Charu. She still remained at home most of the time, more out of fear than by choice. Much to Inaaya's annoyance, her movements had been restricted too. Neel's routine had more or less returned to normal, except that he worked fewer hours, ending his day early to return home.

It was a Tuesday and Neel was at the Bombay Government Hospital as per his routine. As on most Tuesdays, it was a rather slow day at the hospital. A few times over the past years, Neel had even considered discontinuing his pro-bono service, as there were hardly any takers. But he always decided to stick on. *If I can save or change one more life, this will be worth it,* he would manage to convince himself.

He was about to wind up for the day when someone knocked at his door.

'Come in,' Neel said, looking up.

The door opened and a slender woman, not older than thirty, appeared.

'May I come in, doctor?' she asked meekly, her voice barely audible.

Neel smiled and gestured to the chair opposite his. She was dressed in a pink salwar-kameez, her long hair worn in a simple plait. Her face, though pale, was pretty. But despite her fragile appearance and gentle expression, she seemed to exude an inner strength. She placed a worn-out purse on the table in front of her.

'So, how can I help you?' Neel asked her.

She looked at Neel, then down at the floor, uncertainty writ large on her delicate face. It was the same hesitation Neel had seen in many of his patients, especially during their first visits. Twice after entering the room, he could make out, the young woman had almost gotten up and left. But she had summoned the resolve to come to him, and that was half the battle won. So Neel did not push her, instead waiting for her to open up.

Finally, the woman sighed and said, 'I don't want to live anymore, doctor.'

SIXTY-ONE

As she looked up and locked eyes with Neel, he knew she meant it. Neel, with his long experience in dealing with such severe cases, was aware that the first conversation was critical. In most cases, it determined the course of treatment, during which the patient's sense of personal being could either come alive or be destroyed. It was in these first moments that Neel could open the door to the patient's difficult feelings.

'Well, we are not going to let that happen, are we?' he smiled, trying to look as cheerful as he could in front of someone who had just expressed the desire to kill themselves.

She continued to look at Neel, her expression conveying a hint of scepticism.

Neel leaned forward slightly and clasped his hands in front of him.

'Before we start, let me assure you, I am here to *listen* to you, but you can talk freely, as if you are alone. I will do my best to help you; but if at any point during our session, you wish to stop, you may. Okay?'

She nodded.

'Good,' Neel said, his face expressing both concern and interest. 'Can we start with a few basic questions?'

'Yes, doctor.'

'What is your name?'

'Shital Joshi.'

'What do you do, Shital?'

'I have recently started working as a cashier in a local pharmacy, opposite Mahim station, called All-Well 24.'

'I hope you don't mind,' Neel said as he took a sheet of A4 paper from a stack on his desk to make notes. 'Go on, Shital.'

'I came to Mumbai eight years ago from my village in Jalgaon,' Shital said, her eyes tearing up. Neel rose, filled a glass with water from a jug kept handy, and offered it to her. She wiped a tear with a handkerchief clutched in her hand and took a sip.

'I ... actually ... ran away from home ... with Dhiraj. He was not from our village, and my parents were against our relationship.' She paused, waiting for a reaction from Neel. There was none. She continued, 'My nightmare began almost as soon as we reached Mumbai. Dhiraj had no job, no house, nothing ... he didn't even marry me, as he had promised. He was reeling under debt and I took up a job as a maid. And then, the trauma began ...'

For the next thirty minutes, Neel listened intently, making notes intermittently as Shital narrated her ordeal. *The sexual assaults. The violence. By someone she had loved and trusted. Day after day.*

'I felt so numb ... and eventually, I resorted to harming myself, just to feel connected to myself,' she said, rolling up her left sleeve to show him a cut.

And to punish yourself, Neel surmised, and said in a calm, reassuring tone, 'I understand.'

'And now, things have gotten worse,' Shital said.

Neel took a sip of water. *Worse?* He shuddered.

'A month back,' Shital continued, 'he drugged me. When I came to my senses, I saw two other men leaving our house. I am sure that they ... they ... ,' her voice trailed off.

And then, she just wept.

SIXTY-TWO

Neel sat at his desk, staring into nothingness long after Shital left. He had given her anti-depressants, but that would only help her physically. He had to cure her soul.

She had promised to come back the following week. *I hope she does,* Neel sighed.

He looked at his watch; it was almost 7 p.m. He gathered the papers on his desk, put them in his briefcase, and left the hospital. He was conscious of an urgent need to see Charu and Inaaya, just to make sure they were safe.

He saw them lounging in the living room, watching a movie, a big bowl of popcorn between them. Without saying a word, Neel gave them a bear hug each, much to their surprise and amusement.

Neel reached office at his usual time the next morning. Jaya had not yet come in. He went to his cabin, took the papers from his session with Shital out of his bag, and made detailed notes. He liked the old-fashioned method of making notes by hand, instead of using electronic devices. He arranged the set of papers in a new file that he took from a side-drawer, labelled it 'Shital Joshi', and put it on his desk.

He was going through his emails when the door to his cabin opened and Jaya walked in.

'Good morning,' she said, smiling.

'Morning,' Neel said distractedly, typing furiously.

Jaya placed two envelopes on his desk and was leaving the cabin with the rest of the day's mail, when Neel called out to her.

'Jaya, please file this,' he said, handing her Shital's file.

'Sure,' Jaya said, taking the blue file from Neel. She went to the reception, put the stack of envelopes and the file on her desk, and sat down. Just then, Neel's first patient for the day walked in. Jaya greeted her warmly and led her to Neel's cabin.

She knew the session would last an hour. She glanced at the closed door behind her, opened the blue file, and started reading the detailed notes Neel had made.

SIXTY-THREE

'It's been months, Rastogi! And we do not seem to be making any headway in this case,' Commissioner Bedi said.

Rastogi was seated in the commissioner's office, having been summoned at a moment's notice that morning. He had been expecting the call; the press was having a riot lately, calling the Mumbai Police incompetent and slow.

'We are working on it, sir,' Rastogi said.

'I don't care about that. I want the killer to be nabbed,' Bedi snapped uncharacteristically.

'Yes, sir.'

Bedi got up from his chair and walked around his office. Rastogi remained seated, glancing right and left as the Commissioner paced up and down behind him.

Finally, Bedi stopped directly behind Rastogi and put his hands on the Inspector's shoulders. He spoke now in a calm and controlled, though urgent, manner.

'Look, Rastogi, I know you are doing your best. But, it's been months now, and the CM is...'

So, that's where the pressure is coming from, Rastogi realised.

'I will continue following up on the investigation, sir,' Rastogi said, standing up.

'Thank you, Rastogi.'

Rastogi saluted the Commissioner and left his office. *Only a few years to retirement, and I may have to bow out in disgrace,* he thought, as he slowly climbed down two floors, his legs seeming heavier than usual.

SIXTY-FOUR

Neel drove purposefully towards the Bombay Government Hospital. Three weeks and two Tuesdays had passed, and Shital had not turned up since her first visit.

'I hope she makes it today,' Neel thought as he parked his car in the reserved area at the hospital.

He waved to the parking attendant and went up to his consulting room on the third floor. He switched on the air-conditioner, but it refused to start. It was a recurring problem, but Neel had long stopped complaining. He switched on the three-bladed ceiling fan, which soon started wobbling noisily.

Neel wiped the sweat off his forehead and looked at his watch. He dialled the cafeteria and ordered a black coffee with warm milk on the side.

That Tuesday passed too, and there was no sign of Shital.

I hope she has not done something desperate, Neel thought.

SIXTY-FIVE

Jaya got off the local train at Thane station, took the railway bridge and walked eastwards. It was 7 p.m., and the bridge was packed with peak-hour passengers. Clutching the plastic packet close to her chest, she made her way towards the exit; her walk hastened by the continuous nudge of the horde. Instead of taking the stairs at the far end of the bridge, today she went down the steps leading to platforms 4 and 5.

Both platforms were crammed with people. On one side, they were craning their necks, waiting for the next train; on the other, a sea of people were moving towards the staircase, having just disembarked from a train that was chugging slowly out of the station.

As instructed, Jaya walked to a tea-stall below the

indicator and waited. Lost in her thoughts, she jumped at the sound of an oncoming train's horn.

'Did you get it?' A familiar voice asked suddenly, alarming her again.

'Yes ... but I don't think this can go on any longer,' she said.

Ignoring her words, the figure extended a hand, into which Jaya thrust the packet she was carrying. Then, without another word, Manohar disappeared into the crowd.

SIXTY-SIX

It had been a month since he had met Shital—the only time. Neel was getting worried. Once, he considered checking on how she was; he had her phone number. But he decided against it. He had never initiated contact with any of his patients, and he did not want to break that rule.

He returned after a light lunch in the cafeteria at the Bombay Government Hospital and sat down at his desk. The air-conditioner was still not working, but he had reconciled himself to the fact.

There was a soft knock at his door, and a face peeped in. Neel let out a relieved sigh when he realised that it was Shital. 'Please come in, Shital,' he said, making no reference to the visits she had missed.

Almost at once, Neel realised that something was

very wrong. Shital sank into the chair opposite his, looking exhausted and depressed. Aware of Neel's eyes on her, she adjusted her dupatta to cover her neck, but not before he noticed the bruise.

'How are you, Shital? I have been worried about you,' Neel said.

She did not reply.

'What happened? Are you hurt?' Neel continued, indicating her neck. She nodded slowly.

'Dhiraj is forcing me to ...' she stopped, and then continued, 'he brings these men over every night.'

'Why don't you complain to the police?'

'It won't help ... one of them is a cop. And even if they put him behind bars for a while, when he gets out again ...'

'Can't you go back to your parents?'

Shital shook her head, looking down.

'I ... I want this pain to end, doctor. I can't take it anymore,' Shital said, crying softly.

SIXTY-SEVEN

An hour later, Neel escorted Shital out of the consulting room, and walked with her down the passage to the lift. He said goodbye to her as she stepped into the lift, and a sense of doom engulfed him, as though he would never see her again.

As he slowly turned around to return to his room, at the edge of the staircase, he spotted Manohar. He seemed to be arguing with a familiar-looking woman in a nurse's uniform.

'Manohar!' Neel shouted. Manohar's head jerked towards him, and with a look of alarm on his face, he started scrambling down the stairs, two steps at a time. Neel rushed past the nurse, their eyes meeting briefly, and pursued Manohar down the staircase.

Arti Shetye. Neel recollected the name of the nurse

as he reached the first floor. Manohar was gaining ground; Neel had not imagined he could run that fast. The staircase ended in a large concrete courtyard on the ground floor, and when Neel got there, breathing heavily despite his fitness; he was just in time to see Manohar run out of the main gate and disappear.

Neel gave up the chase and dialled Rastogi on his phone.

SIXTY-EIGHT

'So, you are saying you were not in touch with Manohar?' Rastogi asked Arti, narrowing his eyes. They were in Neel's consulting room at the hospital; Neel and Kadam were also present.

'I swear, Inspector. He just came out of nowhere today. I have no idea where he is, or has been, all these days,' Arti said.

'Did he call you?'

'No, you can check my phone,' Arti said promptly, offering her mobile to Rastogi.

'And what were the two of you arguing about?' Neel added.

'Nothing ... I was upset that he disappeared like that ...'

'Did he say where he had been hiding?' Rastogi asked.

'No, he did not say anything about where he had been.'

'And what else did he say?'

'He just said that he had to finish something important, and that everything would be alright.'

SIXTY-NINE

At 11 p.m., the two women employees came out of the All-Well 24 pharmacy, their shift over. The lone staff member inside the shop pulled the shutter down from the inside. The shutter, which covered the whole entrance to the pharmacy, had a separate, 2' by 2' hinged frame at its centre. It had the same stiles and rails as the shutter, and could be opened to service customers—give medicines and collect cash—between 11 p.m. and 7 a.m. Earlier, the pharmacy had never lowered its shutter at night, but increasing incidents of armed robberies in the area had forced the owner to implement the safety measure.

Shital and her colleague walked together for around a hundred metres. Then her colleague waved goodbye and crossed the road to Mahim station. Shital walked slowly, almost reluctantly, home. In another five minutes, she turned left into a narrow, deserted lane, lit by dim streetlights. Apart from a taxi that was parked in a corner, there were no other vehicles.

The hooded figure, following Shital, kept a safe distance of around fifty metres. As Shital made a turn to the right, the figure stopped and waited at the corner, knowing there was a dead-end just a block away. There were six two-storeyed buildings on either side, all of them dilapidated and dark. A street dog roaming nearby made its way towards the waiting figure, who prayed it would not bark. The dog's attention was diverted when it spotted a discarded paper bag and trotted off in the opposite direction.

Shital slowed her pace and entered the last building on the right. There was only one room on the second floor where the lights were on, like a yellow box suspended in the black night. The hooded figure moved forward, eyes on the building, waiting to see if the lights in another room were switched on. They didn't. But after a few minutes, a woman's shadow passed across the closed, lit window. It was Shital.

The hooded figure now moved quickly forward and entered the unwelcoming edifice. A narrow wooden staircase ran up the building. A single bulb glowed dimly on the first-floor landing. The figure waited for a moment to transfer the iron rod to the left hand, and then, holding the dusty railing with the right, slowly climbed up to the second floor.

SEVENTY

The hooded figure reached the second level and walked on the unevenly tiled floor towards Shital's room. It was not difficult to identify it, as noises could be heard from inside. A loud thumping sound, followed by the shrill echoes of a woman's scream.

The figure stood outside the door for a moment, put the black mask on underneath the hoodie, and then knocked on the flimsy wooden door. The commotion inside stopped almost at once, and a male voice shouted, 'Who is it?'

Silence.

'Who is it?' The voice repeated.

Shuffling footsteps broke the silence, and then the door was clumsily unlocked. It slowly creaked open, and Shital screamed again upon seeing the masked figure, who kicked the door wide open and came in, hands clasping an iron rod.

The frail man inside the room, dressed in shorts and a vest, shrieked and ran to the adjoining room. The masked figure followed him. The door was ajar, and it was completely dark inside. The figure hesitantly stepped into the room, and the lights came on.

'Got you,' Rastogi said, pointing a revolver.

SEVENTY-ONE

'You cannot hide from me,' the voice said.
The construction site was covered with loose soil, a few small trees at the far end. Temporary access had been created after the demolition of the earlier structure. Concrete columns extended up to the first level over the entire plot. Dark, cold walls ran along one side, connecting some of the columns. It was a moonless night, and the teenager groped along the wall, moving forward, away from the menacing voice.

'Where are you?' The voice screamed angrily.

The young heart was beating furiously now, frightened that its own sound might give it away. *When will I stop running? Will this ever end?* And maybe, at that moment, the decision was made.

'You are going to suffer when I catch you,' the menacing voice trembled with rage.

The iron rod was gripped tightly in two young hands, waiting for Uncle to come closer.

The shadow appeared from behind a pillar. It crossed the pillar and stood for a moment, looking around, hands on hips. On a concrete slab in front of him, it saw another shadow creeping up behind him, and turned around.

At the exact moment, the iron rod came crashing into his skull.

The kid stood over the dead man for a few minutes, soaking in the relief as well as the dread of what had just happened. As the enormity of the situation dawned, the young legs jerked backwards, stumbling and falling head down on a pile of bricks.

SEVENTY-TWO

Instinctively, at the memory, Neel tried to touch the scar on his temple, but couldn't. He heard the handcuffs rattle behind his back, and came back to reality. He was in the backseat of a police car; he could see Shital's building out the window to his left, and flurry of activity below it. Inspector Rastogi was speaking to someone on his mobile phone; Kadam and the frail man he had seen in Shital's house were chatting animatedly. *And Shital, where was she?* He was still worried about her.

Just then, he saw Shital come down the staircase, but she was no longer the meek and gentle woman he had been trying to protect. She now walked confidently, upright, with a steely look on her face. She walked over to Rastogi and saluted him, who in turn gave her a thumbs-up sign. *Well done.*

Neel shook his head and let out a short laugh.

SEVENTY-THREE

Neel was seated opposite Rastogi in the interrogation room of the Wadala Police Station. The windowless room was bare except for a desk with two chairs on one side and one more on the other.

Neel had offered to give a full confession in return for a 'no-media' trial. Rastogi had used his influence with the Commissioner to accept the deal. After some consideration, the Commissioner had agreed.

Neel stared at his handcuffs, and then looked up at the magistrate seated next to Rastogi. He remembered reading somewhere that a confession made to a police officer is inadmissible in court; hence, a magistrate was often present during interrogations for the purpose of recording these statements.

The magistrate started by explaining to Neel that he was not bound to give a confession. Neel cut her short and gave his consent, urging them to get on with the procedure.

Why? That was what Rastogi was most eager to know. *The motive.*

They took a break after two hours, during which Rastogi had listened with rapt attention as the magistrate recorded a detailed statement on her notepad. She left the room briefly, and Rastogi waited for the door to close before he spoke.

'For whatever it is worth, I am sorry to hear about what you had to endure in your childhood.'

Neel nodded, looking at the floor.

'How are Charu and Inaaya?' he asked, his voice choking.

'As promised, I met Mrs Burman personally ... obviously, she is shattered. Inaaya does not know yet ... Mrs Burman said she would handle it later,' Rastogi said.

Neel pursed his lips and looked up at Rastogi. In spite of the circumstances, he could not help but admire the policeman. He had kept his word.

The door opened; the magistrate walked in and took

her seat next to Rastogi. She opened her folder, turned to a fresh page and neatly numbered it '14' at the top.

'Shall we continue?' she asked, looking at Rastogi and Neel.

SEVENTY-FOUR

'And the post-its? Were you expressing regret for what you had done?' The magistrate asked Neel.

'No, not at all. I have no regrets; the bastards deserved to die after what they had done to Nitya and Arti. I wish I could identify more of them and—' Neel did not feel the need to complete the sentence.

'But as a doctor, your job is to save lives, not to take them,' the magistrate said.

'You still don't get it, do you?' Neel smirked. 'I *did* save lives.'

'But why the "*Sorry*" on the post-its then?' Rastogi asked.

'It was an apology from *them* … for what they had done.'

SEVENTY-FIVE

Rastogi and Kadam drove in silence as the car headed towards the police headquarters. Rastogi had been summoned to debrief the Commissioner, after Neel's confession.

'Sir, may I ask a question?' Kadam spoke, finally.

Rastogi nodded, his sombre gaze meeting Kadam's.

'What made you think that Dr Burman could be the killer?' Kadam asked.

'My suspicions were jogged after the attack on Mrs Burman. Had the killer actually wanted to, it would not have been too difficult to kill her, but she escaped. *How?* I asked myself. And the most likely answer was, *because the attacker wanted her to escape.*

'After that,' Rastogi continued, 'I began pursuing the

case in a different light. The two missing files further reinforced my new line of thinking.'

Kadam gave his boss a confused look. Rastogi went on, 'Dr Burman had as much access to the files as Manohar or Jaya. If anything in the files had pointed to Manohar, Dr Burman would have known, and he would have alerted the police or confronted Manohar. He did neither.'

'But … why did Manohar disappear? I mean, he has been acting strangely all along,' exclaimed Kadam.

'Manohar is a habitual gambler, and he owed a considerable sum of money to some very … umm … let's say, avoidable characters. When things got really ugly, he fled. Scared of losing the woman he loved—Arti—he could not stay away and visited her at the hospital.'

'But … how do you know all this, sir?'

'From the man himself! Manohar met me soon after the hospital incident; he was scared and wanted to clarify that he had nothing to do with the murders. He wanted to make a fresh beginning, get married … and Jaya had promised to bail him out with some cash she had saved … which, I think, she did.'

Kadam parked the car in the compound at the police headquarters, and both he and Rastogi got out.

'I will wait here, sir,' Kadam said. Rastogi smiled and nodded as he walked towards the commissioner's office.

'Sir,' Kadam called out; Rastogi turned.

Kadam saluted him.

SEVENTY-SIX

Six months had passed since Neel's arrest and his subsequent sentencing to life imprisonment. He did not appeal against the decision.

The Crossword bookstore at Kemps Corner in South Mumbai was packed to its full capacity. A long queue of readers had formed to get the bestseller signed by the author. Charu signed the books willingly, writing personalised messages and even posing for pictures.

Rastogi waited patiently at the end of the line. He saw Manohar and Arti, now man and wife, and smiled at them. Inaaya, accompanied by Jaya, was interacting with the guests. Finally, when the last of the invitees had left, Rastogi went up to Charu. Inaaya was by her side.

Rastogi smiled and handed his copy over to Charu, who laughed. As she was signing the copy, Rastogi looked at Inaaya, and said, 'I am glad to see you.'

Inaaya smiled at him affectionately. Rastogi had been a pillar of strength for both mother and daughter, along with Jaya and Manohar.

'I wish Dad was here,' Inaaya said, teary-eyed.

Rastogi had made up the story of Neel's car accident, in which he had lost his life, and neither the body nor the car could be recovered. He remembered going through the details, in case Inaaya asked, with Charu, Manohar and Jaya. The co-conspirators exchanged a silent, knowing glance. Their secret would stay buried forever.

Rastogi smiled and put his hand on Inaaya's head. He then said goodbye, and slowly made his way out of the bookstore.

ABOUT THE AUTHOR

Ravi Subramanian is the award-winning author of ten novels. His stories are set against the backdrop of the financial services industry. He has won the Economist Crossword Book Award three years in a row, as well as the Golden Quill Readers' Choice Award. His books have been translated into Hindi, Tamil and Latvian. Visit him at www.subramanianravi.com or connect with him on Twitter @subramanianravi or on Instagram @Ravisubramanian70.

Jigs Ashar is an award-winning writer and banker-turned-consultant. His first short story, *The Wait is Killing* was adjudged a winner by Jeffrey Archer in the *Times of India–Write India Season 2* contest; and his second, *Make(up) in India*, chosen by Shobhaa De, was also a winner in the same season. His third story, *Duel*, was shortlisted for the *Juggernaut Short Story Prize* for the year 2018.

After nineteen years with leading MNC banks, Jigs took the plunge into writing after getting a certification in Creative Writing from Xavier Institute of Communications. He currently works as a consultant with the World Bank Group. He is also an avid marathoner.

Jigs lives in Mumbai with his wife, Vidya, and daughter, Esha. You can follow him on Twitter @JigneshAshar1 and on Instagram @jigsashar.

30 Years *of*
HarperCollins *Publishers* India

At HarperCollins, we believe in telling the best stories and finding the widest possible readership for our books in every format possible. We started publishing 30 years ago; a great deal has changed since then, but what has remained constant is the passion with which our authors write their books, the love with which readers receive them, and the sheer joy and excitement that we as publishers feel in being a part of the publishing process.

Over the years, we've had the pleasure of publishing some of the finest writing from the subcontinent and around the world, and some of the biggest bestsellers in India's publishing history. Our books and authors have won a phenomenal range of awards, and we ourselves have been named Publisher of the Year the greatest number of times. But nothing has meant more to us than the fact that millions of people have read the books we published, and somewhere, a book of ours might have made a difference.

As we step into our fourth decade, we go back to that one word – a word which has been a driving force for us all these years.

Read.

Harper Collins | 4th | HARPER PERENNIAL | HARPER BUSINESS | HARPER BLACK | हार्पर हिन्दी

HarperCollins *Children'sBooks* | HARPER DESIGN | HARPER VANTAGE | Harper Sport